Threads of Hope

The Coleman Series

Katie Winters

Chapter One

As early September sunlight streamed through the convertible windows, Oriana Coleman realized that her little sister, Meghan, had begun to look almost exactly like their mother, Mia. With her head flung back, laughing at a joke Oriana had just made, her eyes danced just as their mother's had; the long sweep of her neck was the same, and even her laugh was like an echo of Mia's. A swell of nostalgia overcame Oriana, and she struggled to breathe for a moment. They'd lost their mother many years ago now. Oriana and Meghan were all that was left of her memory.

"What are you thinking about?" Meghan had noticed Oriana's reverie.

Oriana twitched into a smile. "Nothing! Nothing. Just nervous about tomorrow, I guess."

Meghan adjusted her glasses on the bridge of her nose. "It's hard for me to believe you ever get nervous."

"Don't tell anyone," Oriana joked. "I try to maintain sophistication in all things."

"Your secret is safe with me," Meghan said.

Oriana and Meghan were halfway to New York City, where Oriana had several meetings with important clients, plus a party where she planned to rub shoulders with artists and other potential buyers. For more than twenty-five years, Oriana had worked as a high-end art dealer and had been responsible for some of the most towering sales of the twenty-first century. After her first few years cutting her teeth in New York City, she'd made enough of a name for herself to move home to Martha's Vineyard to be near Meghan, her father, and her mother and raise her children. Although she'd occasionally missed the hustle and bustle of the city, being an "island art dealer" had come in her favor, as she'd had a bit of mystique. Plus, plenty of New Yorkers vacationed in Nantucket or Martha's Vineyard, and they required her assistance to decorate their homes with exquisite art to impress their friends.

"I can't remember the last time we were off the island together," Meghan said. "Miami, maybe? Or that trip to Seattle?"

"It must have been Nashville," Oriana remembered. "I met that client to sell an Aronski sculpture."

"That's right! And after you sealed the deal, we went out and sang karaoke." Meghan snapped her fingers.

"Oh. That hangover nearly killed me," Oriana said. "What song did I sing at the end of the night?"

"You sang Prince!" Meghan cackled. "'When Doves Cry.' You brought down the house."

"My finest moment," Oriana added, rolling her eyes. "Thank goodness none of my clients saw me up there. They would never trust a crazy woman like that to handle their art deals."

"On the contrary, I'd trust someone like that even more," Meghan quipped.

Outside the convertible windows, a glistening September day surged past, fields tinged with brown yet still clinging to the fertile greenery of summer. There was something so devastating about the end of summer, a reminder that life was limited, that you only had so much time to love, feel, and breathe.

"I got a text from Sam," Meghan interrupted Oriana's reverie again. "She says Hilary's surgery went well. She's out and resting at home."

Oriana breathed a sigh of relief. "I'm so glad to hear that."

"Can you imagine losing your vision? What a nightmare."

"Especially because she works in design," Oriana added, stricken.

Hilary Coleman, who'd just had surgery to treat her glaucoma, was Meghan and Oriana's half-niece, the daughter of their half-brother Roland Coleman. For a very long time, Meghan and Oriana had known of the existence of their older Nantucket half-brothers, Roland and Grant— yet they'd also known they weren't to approach them. Their father, Chuck Coleman, had cheated on his first wife to such a degree that he'd begun a second family with Meghan and Oriana's mother— without divorcing her. When Roland and Grant had discovered his secret, Chuck had bribed them not to tell. But as a result, Roland and Grant decided to cut Chuck out of their lives forever. Roland and Grant's best-laid plans had blown up in their faces, however, when Roland's daughter, Samantha, had found a series of diaries from her Great Aunt Jessabelle, in which Jess-abelle had written the dramatic details of Chuck's affair.

Over the previous summer, the two sides of the Coleman Family had slowly come together— everyone except Roland and Grant, of course, who still partially blamed Oriana and Meghan for their mother's death. This, of course, wasn't fair, as, back then, Oriana and Meghan had been children, unversed in family dramas and heartache.

Oriana had booked them two suites in the gorgeous Dominick Hotel in Greenwich Village, the hotel she frequented on her many trips to New York per year. The fact that Meghan could tag along this time pleased her. Traveling was better with someone you loved by your side. So often, Oriana had sat all by herself in Central Park, at a beautiful restaurant, or in a museum, wishing she could talk about her experiences with someone.

Oriana and Meghan got out of the convertible at the hotel entrance, where Oriana handed off the keys to a valet driver, and a bellhop took their suitcases. Around them, the city was alive, loud, and panic-stricken. Taxis beeped and honked as the street seemed to shake, possibly with the weight of a subway train underground, and the smells were a mix of garbage, hot dogs, and concrete. There was a reason Oriana wanted to live in Martha's Vineyard— she remembered it every time she came into the city. Still, there was no refuting the city's magic. It was everywhere you looked.

Oriana and Meghan parted when they reached their suites, deciding to rest up for an hour before they grabbed dinner and went for a walk. Inside her room, Oriana stretched out on the king-sized bed, thinking how nice it was sometimes to stay in hotels and feel anonymous in a huge city.

Oriana grabbed her phone and called her husband, Reese. His deep baritone voice came through the speaker a moment later, her anchor in any storm. He sounded happy.

"Hi, honey. Did you make it?"

"We did." Oriana curled into a ball on the bed and cupped her phone to her ear, trying to feel like Reese was closer than he was. "And the hotel is just as beautiful as ever."

"I'm so glad to hear that."

"What are you up to?"

"Well, Benny and I are about to head outside for another round of baseball," Reese explained.

Oriana's heart filled with love. Benny was their three-year-old grandson, the only son of their daughter, Alexa. Over the past year, they'd been lost in a nightmare, as Benny had been diagnosed with cancer and gone through treatment after treatment. Miraculously, Benny had been cured that summer and transformed into a boisterous little boy again. Oriana and Reese were often so thankful that it brought them to tears.

"That boy can't get enough of playing baseball with Grandpa," Oriana said.

"Yeah! He almost caught the ball a few times earlier," Reese said.

"Progress!"

After Reese and Oriana got off the phone, Oriana went to the bathroom to brush her teeth and touch up her makeup. Meghan texted to say she needed a little more time to prep before dinner and asked if they could meet at seven-thirty instead. Oriana said of course. There was no rush.

There was a knock at the door. Oriana walked toward it without thinking twice and opened it to find another bellhop with a tray upon which sat a bottle of champagne, a glass, and an envelope with Oriana's name on it.

"Special delivery," the bellhop said.

"Oh wow! Thank you." Oriana opened the door wider so the bellhop could enter and place the tray on the table.

"Have a wonderful stay." The bellhop beamed and left as quickly as he'd come. The door fell back into place, leaving Oriana alone with the champagne, which she uncorked expertly to pour herself a half glass. This was a new edition to the Dominick Hotel stay— one she welcomed, especially after such a long drive. With her flute in her hand, she raised it toward the window, through which she could see across Manhattan, then drank.

Oriana then remembered the envelope. Her first hunch was that it was a coupon for the hotel restaurant or bar or perhaps a note thanking her for continuing to choose the Dominick Hotel for her many visits. In fact, she considered just tossing it into the trash, if only because it didn't seem to matter to her.

But instead, she opened it, pulled out a notecard, and read:

I know what you did in 1998.

Immediately, Oriana's heart burst with fear, and she felt her pulse quicken. She stood to her feet, reading and rereading the message, which had been typed out, perhaps with a typewriter. It looked like something from a crime novel.

Oh gosh. Who was it from? They couldn't possibly know. This must be about something else.

Suddenly, there was another knock on the door. This time, Oriana was petrified, and she hardly heard her voice as she cried out, "Who is it?"

"Oriana? It's Meghan!"

Oriana shook as she walked to the door. When she opened it, Meghan's smile instantly fell off her face.

"What's wrong?"

Oriana bristled. "Did the hotel send you a bottle of champagne?"

"What! No."

Oriana glanced back at the champagne, fearing she'd been poisoned. But the cork had been in the bottle. The glass had seemed clean.

"I guess they know you made the reservation," Meghan said with a laugh, entering the room.

"Is it already seven-thirty?" Oriana asked, her throat very tight.

"Five minutes past," Meghan said.

Oriana scratched her head. *How had so much time passed since Meghan had texted?* It felt like she'd lost much of her life, presumably due to fear.

"They only sent me one glass," Oriana said, deftly pocketing the sinister notecard before Meghan could see it.

"That's okay," Meghan said. "Why don't we go out? I'm starving."

"Great idea, I'm famished," Oriana agreed, although she wasn't sure she'd be able to eat.

As Oriana followed Meghan into the hallway toward the elevator, her heartbeat burst in her ears. She rolled through horrific images from all those years ago— a time

7

when everything in her life had been in flux, and she'd allowed a lie to become enormous. Now, it seemed, the lie had gotten so big that it had decided to come back from the past and swallow her whole.

There was no way she would recover from this. If her secret came to the surface, her future would be destroyed.

Chapter Two

That night and the following morning, Oriana did her best to play the part of a happy, confident older sister— the woman Meghan knew. Throughout, she swam with fears and suspicions and frequently had to sneak off to the bathroom to hyperventilate.

The worst thing about receiving this notecard was that she didn't know what the person planned next. They knew what she'd done, but how would they use it against her? When would they strike? Or were they willing to talk it out, learn why she'd done what she'd done, and back off— perhaps for a sum of money? What would stop this person from revealing her secret?

Oriana and Meghan decided to go to the Museum of Modern Art after lunch, before Oriana's first meeting with a rich client. As they walked through the grand rooms, assessing modern art, Oriana found it difficult to appreciate anything. In fact, she'd begun to look at the people in the museum instead. It occurred to her that whoever sent the card had tracked her down at the

Dominick Hotel— which meant they were following her in some capacity. *Were they tracking her, even now?*

Toward a big red sculpture, a man with gray hair and glasses eyed her and tugged his ear. *Was that a signal?* On the other side of the room, a woman in a magenta dress frowned suspiciously. Did Oriana recognize these people from anywhere? *Were they from her past?*

"You've been so quiet today," Meghan said, not unkindly. "Still nervous about later?"

"I guess so," Oriana lied. "Geoffrey is a difficult client to please. I researched extensively for him, but I have doubts he'll like any of it."

"But you have other meetings lined up this week," Meghan pointed out. "So, it's not like the trip is a waste if you don't sell to him."

"Right." Oriana nodded in agreement.

After the museum, Oriana and Meghan parted ways for the day. Meghan was off to see an old friend from high school who lived in the city, and Oriana had her client meeting, followed by the artsy party with high-rolling dealers and fantastic artists. Oriana hugged Meghan a little too hard as they parted.

"You promise you're okay?" Meghan asked, locking her gaze with Oriana's.

"I'm totally fine," Oriana assured her. "Go. Have fun. I'm jealous you don't have to go to this swanky party. I'm sure there will be many pretentious people talking about nothing at all."

"They'll adore you," Meghan said. "At least you're not boring like they are."

"If you say so."

Oriana watched Meghan walk down the road, her trench coat whipping in the wind before she disappeared around the corner. Then, Oriana turned around, eyeing each and every person on the street, standing outside the bodega, and across from her, at the park. *Had any of them been inside the museum with her? Did any of them seem suspicious?*

Oh gosh. She was losing her mind.

Oriana's client meeting was held on West 71st Street at a very old apartment with high ceilings and exposed brick. The man who owned it was Geoffrey Thompkins, and he'd used Oriana as his exclusive art dealer for the previous twenty years— since they'd met at a party held by the then-owner of the Mets. Geoffrey had been struck by Oriana's wit and art knowledge and had hired her to purchase art for his new apartment, this very one. Since then, he'd needed frequent updates as he grew bored of looking at the same art every day. Oriana was pleased to help, even if his arrogance got on her nerves sometimes.

"Welcome, Oriana." Geoffrey kissed her on both cheeks, probably because he spent too much time in France every year, and opened the door wider to let her in. Just as he often did, Geoffrey had covered several paintings on the wall with cloths, as they'd gotten so boring that they "hurt his eyes."

"I see you've fallen into the same old trap, Geoffrey," Oriana teased him as she sat on his chaise longue and crossed her ankles.

"The colors of that Henrietta painting began to burn my pupils, Oriana," Geoffrey said.

Oriana bristled with annoyance, thinking of her half-niece, Hilary, whose eyes had genuinely failed her. Geoffrey's jokes weren't funny.

"I'm sure we can find something that suits you," Oriana said, studying Geoffrey's face, ornate glasses, and thick beard. *Was that a flicker in his eye? Did he know something about the note she'd received yesterday?* After all, he'd known she was coming to New York City for quite some time at this point. Perhaps he'd told whoever this was that she always stayed at the Dominick Hotel. Or perhaps he was the one who had the information in the first place. *But why would he use that information now? What good would it do him?* Plus, he had more money than God.

Trying to push her fears aside, Oriana brought out her portfolio to show off the various fresh artwork she now dealt with— most of which were priced in the millions. Looking vaguely bored, Geoffrey went through them, selected six or seven at random, and then instructed her to sell three pieces he no longer wanted. Normally, Oriana would have been thrilled, but nothing about this day could please her.

"I'll see you at the party this evening?" Geoffrey asked as she stood to leave.

"I'll be there."

"Wonderful. I always find those people so boring."

Oriana wanted to point out that he was one of the most boring people to attend, but she kept her mouth shut.

Back in the hotel suite, Oriana sat and stared at the notecard for a long time, her heart thudding. Nothing about the card gave any indication of who it was from. She supposed if this was a crime thriller, the person receiving the card would find a clue— a dash of blue paint on the notecard that suggested the person was a painter, or even the type of print, which perhaps could show what kind of typewriter had been used. But Oriana was just an art dealer. She had never read any Sherlock Holmes books.

For the party that night, Oriana dressed in a simple yet sophisticated black dress and styled her short blond hair so that it was especially shiny and sleek. A taxi pulled up just as she left the hotel, and she slipped into the back-seat wearing a smile as she said the address of the party.

The taxi pulled outside the apartment building on the Upper West Side at half-past nine. Oriana paid the driver and stepped out of the car, where a doorman immediately greeted her and allowed her entry. Plenty of other beauti-fully dressed people were coming in for the party— it was clear she was one of them.

Still, Oriana felt uneasy, carrying such a long-lost secret that could potentially expose her past— ruin every-thing she worked so hard for in the blink of an eye.

The party that evening was held by the B-celebrity actress Monica Streetwise, who'd risen to fame during her twenties in a hit sitcom called *All About My Brother* before following that up with romantic comedies that had slight "edges" to them. Now, in her forties, Monica's roles had more-or-less dried up, but she had enough sitcom money to roll with the high artists of New York City. None of them let her know how much they looked down on her for her role in that sitcom, as they appreciated her lavish parties too much.

Oriana didn't know Monica well, but she did rather like her. She appreciated when Monica made fun of her sitcom, saying that it "paid the bills," which was what it was meant to do. Although Oriana existed in the "upper echelon" of the art world, she understood that sometimes, Americans just wanted to sit on the couch and watch a sitcom. Sometimes, people just wanted to relax and not "engage" with high art.

Oriana entered the luxurious apartment and was immediately handed a glass of champagne, which she sipped slowly, not wanting to get drunk. Not when there was so much at stake. Immediately, one of her clients approached her, eager to discuss an art piece they craved. Oriana instantly went into business mode, grateful to think about something besides her fears.

But after her client left to speak to someone else, Oriana stood alone momentarily, scanning the crowd, eyeing their beautifully made clothing, expensive hair-cuts, and the way they spoke to one another, all pretending to be a lot more charming than they were. Oriana would have preferred to be in Martha's Vineyard, surrounded by her family and friends. They certainly laughed a lot more.

Then again, even if she did make it home, whoever knew her secret probably knew where she lived. Nervous, she placed her barely drunk champagne glass to the side and weaved through the crowd, trying to keep tabs on everyone.

"Oriana!"

Oriana spun at the sound of her name to watch as an old, dear friend of hers approached through the crowd. Nick Walters was handsome, successful, and sharp as a tack. Oriana had met him during her New York City years before she'd been able to move her entire family back to Martha's Vineyard.

"Nick Walters! My gosh." Oriana hugged him and immediately relaxed into herself, remembering the person she'd been all those years ago— before everything had happened.

"I saw you from across the party and thought, 'Who is that glamorous woman standing alone?' And then, I realized, it was you!" Nick laughed. "When was the last time we saw each other?"

"Gosh, it's been too long, Nick." Oriana furrowed her brow, trying to add up the years. "How have you been?"

Nick explained he'd been traveling for work a lot recently, that he'd been in Beijing, Bangkok, and Budapest, but he'd craved the comforts of New York City and was so glad to be back.

"I don't know how you ever left, Oriana," Nick said.

Oriana sighed. "I know. But I couldn't have raised Joel and Alexa here."

"I always forget that you're a mother, first and foremost," Nick said. "I suppose the couture clothing always throws me off."

Oriana laughed. "I have plenty of mom jeans at home. Mark my words."

"Honey, don't talk about mom jeans here," Nick hissed playfully. "They might kick you out of the party!"

Oriana's heart lifted at the banter with her dear friend. For a little while, she allowed herself to fall into the glitz of the night, even drinking a glass of champagne and allowing Nick to guide her through the party to chat with guests she hadn't met before. But by the time eleven-thirty hit, Oriana's fears had returned, and she admitted to Nick that she was in the midst of a "family emergency" and needed to get back to the hotel.

Nick was noticeably disappointed. "I hate to hear that, honey. Can I help you with anything?"

"You're sweet," Oriana said. "But this is something I have to deal with on my own, I'm afraid."

"You were always too strong for your own good," Nick said.

Oriana said goodbye to everyone she'd spoken with, then slipped into the wild New York City night, taking a taxi back toward her hotel. A few blocks prior to it, she asked the taxi to drop her off, as she hadn't eaten a proper dinner, and she wanted to grab a few snacks at a bodega— fruit, maybe pretzels and guacamole. Anything to tide her over till tomorrow.

But as Oriana stood in line at the cash register, carrying her goods, a man walked into the bodega. Oriana's heart stopped beating. His face was familiar. Too familiar.

He'd been at the party.

Outraged, Oriana placed her goods on the counter and marched directly up to him. His eyes widened with surprise.

"Why did you follow me?" Oriana demanded, crossing her arms over her chest.

The man stuttered. "Pardon?"

"I said, why did you follow me from the party? I remember you. And I know what you're up to. You aren't going to get away with this."

The man tilted his head, and his eyes swam with confusion. *He was a brilliant actor. He should have won an award.*

"Come on," Oriana blurted. "Who told you? How did you find out?" After all, as far as Oriana knew, only one person in the world knew what had happened in 1998— and that person's name was Brea. But Oriana hadn't seen Brea since the year 2000. She imagined she never would again.

But the man staggered away from her, raising his

hands. "Listen, lady. I don't know who you are. I was at a party, sure. But I don't remember you being there."

Oriana flared her nostrils. "Just tell me what you want. Please, I can't stand being followed. I can't stand all the games."

But the man continued to back out of the bodega. "I don't want anything from you! I'm staying at a hotel down the road, and I just came in to get a snack. I swear." He continued to shake his head, then removed his wallet from his back pocket and handed her his ID. "I don't even live here. I'm from Minnesota. A friend from high school used to date Monica, and he invited me to the party."

Oriana gaped at the ID, which showed a younger version of the man before her, wearing glasses and a salmon polo shirt. The address was Minneapolis, Minnesota.

Oriana wasn't sure what to believe. She felt herself going insane. Slowly, she passed back the ID, wanting to threaten him, to tell him that if she saw him again, she would call the police. *But what proof did she have?*

Abandoning her snacks, Oriana walked back into the night and hurried to Meghan's suite, where she knocked on the door until a sleepy Meghan answered and asked if everything was okay.

"Can I sleep in your bed tonight?" Oriana asked, hating how pathetic she sounded. This was exactly what Meghan had done to Oriana as a kid when Oriana's three years on Meghan had seemed like forever.

"Of course," Meghan said, stepping back. "Is everything all right?"

"Yes," Oriana breathed. "It's just that, you know, the suite is too big for one person. I felt alone."

Meghan shrugged, too tired to ask additional ques-

17

tions, then clambered back into bed. Oriana donned one of Meghan's oversized sleep shirts and slipped in beside her, staring through the darkness as Meghan's breathing calmed and deepened. Oriana wasn't sure if she would ever sleep well again.

Something terrible was about to happen. She felt her world was about to crumble, and she had no control over it.

Chapter Three

The Island of Ko Tao, Thailand

Brea settled into a downward dog position, her hands flat on the mat as she breathed in, breathed out. Around her, women in tight shorts and tank tops did the same, their arms and legs glistening from sweat. The heat on the island was nearly ninety degrees, despite the earliness of the morning, but Brea had been in Thailand for many years now. Her skin was almost used to it.

The woman who ran the yoga studio was also American, but she'd lived in Thailand for thirty years and therefore spoke perfect Thai. She said goodbye to women as they left, easily switching between Thai and English, as though she hardly noticed the change.

"Brea, good to see you again!" The teacher smiled eagerly and placed her hands on her hips.

Brea stalled at the door, clutching her yoga mat. This wasn't the first time the yoga teacher had tried to get chummy with her. Brea was the only other American woman who lived alone on Ko Tao— at least, she was the only one she knew of. It stood to reason that she and the yoga instructor should become friends. The only problem was that Brea had no idea how to make friends anymore. She'd lost all her socializing skills.

"Yeah! Great class," Brea said hurriedly. "Um. Thank you. See you next time."

Before the yoga teacher could answer, Brea fled the yoga studio and jumped on her motorbike, which sputtered as it took her downtown, where a food market sold fresh fruits, vegetables, and various dishes all day long. There, Brea bought mangoes, fresh fish, and a little snack made of red bean paste, which was strangely sweet. Back on Martha's Vineyard, where she'd grown up, a snack like this would have been deemed "bizarre." Brea had come to love it.

Ko Tao was surrounded by pristine, turquoise water that was oddly warm, especially when compared to the ocean of her youth. At the beach, she stripped to her swimsuit and swam out, floating on her back as she studied the gorgeous sky above. Thailand weather was almost continually beautiful, which made it difficult for her to comprehend the changing seasons. Sometimes, she had to remind herself that she was fifty years old— that she'd lived a large part of her life. Sometimes, that brought her to tears, especially when she considered that she couldn't return to Martha's Vineyard, perhaps ever again.

Brea dried off after her swim, jumped back on the motorbike, and sped back to her little house, which had a living room, kitchen, bedroom, and not much more. Over the years, she'd learned to make her life simple. She had an e-reader, which allowed her to purchase books online and not bother with three-dimensional books. She also had a laptop to watch movies and TV shows. With so many books and films to discover, she could almost convince herself that she didn't need the rest of the world.

Around noon, Brea's neighbor, a Thai woman named Chailai, knocked on her door and delivered her a fresh plate of Pad Thai— one of Brea's favorite dishes.

"Thank you," Brea said in Thai, overwhelmed with the constant generosity of her neighbor. Chailai clearly felt bad for her and thought Brea being alone at her age was inappropriate and just plain sad. All she could do was throw food at her, perhaps as a way to comfort her.

"Would you like to come over?" Chailai asked, her eyebrows high.

"Oh. Um. I don't think so. Thank you," Brea stammered in Thai, always embarrassed to speak another language.

Chailai shrugged, at a loss, then waved and turned back as Brea said, "I'll bring back the plate later!" It was their consistent dance.

Back in the air conditioning, Brea sat at the kitchen table, put on a podcast, and twirled her Pad Thai around and around her fork, eating slowly to savor every bite. Oh, she loved this food! Growing up, she hadn't known such Asian flavors existed. Her life had been a constant rotation of fresh fish, mashed potatoes, and clam chowder. Her mother had been a wonderful cook and had tried her darndest to pass on that knowledge to Brea, but Brea had been driven in other directions and never bothered to get half as good.

As Brea cleaned the rest of her plate, her phone dinged. It was an email. Normally, Brea's emails were from websites, advertising sales, or spam.

But this time, the email was very different. It nearly knocked the wind out of her chest.

Brea,

I have absolutely no idea where you are, but regardless, I need you to contact me immediately. We need to talk.

Oriana

Brea stared at the message for a long time, her mouth still full of noodles she'd forgotten to chew.

Why was Oriana reaching out to her after twenty-three years of silence? What was going on?

At first, Brea tried to write her a message. She watched her shaking fingers compose several words:

Oriana, wow. Happy to hear from you. Um.

But then, she deleted the message as her heart filled with rage. Oriana hadn't reached out to her due to kindness. Something else had happened. And Brea didn't want anything to do with it. She'd come to Thailand for a reason. And she knew that Oriana couldn't track her down— mostly because she had a system in place to ensure that she couldn't be found. That had taken some serious acrobatics in terms of IDs and money transfers, but it had protected her.

But with Oriana's email in her mind, Brea wasn't sure what to do with her body. She felt anxious and jittery, so she stood up, cleaned her neighbor's plate in the sink, then jumped back on her motorbike. As she sped down the road, going faster and faster, she let out a horrible scream.

After nearly an hour of aimless riding, Brea was exhausted. She stopped at a downtown bar near the beach, where she sat sweating and ordered a Tiger beer. The guy behind the counter was called Fox, which was probably not his real name. She'd met him several times at this bar and always appreciated his quietness. He didn't mind leaving her to her thoughts.

But today, because of Oriana's email, Brea needed someone to talk to.

"What's going on, Fox?" Brea hardly recognized her voice. It had been a long time since she'd started small talk.

Fox dried a beer glass with a towel and smiled. "Not much, man. Nothing goes on here in Ko Tao. I guess that's part of the appeal, isn't it?"

Brea nodded. "Do you ever get bored of that?"

"Of the fact that every single day feels the same as the one before?"

Brea laughed in spite of herself.

"I mean, sure," Fox said.

"And do you ever think about going back to wherever you came from?" Brea asked.

Fox raised his eyebrows. "Do you?"

Brea sipped her beer, sensing that she'd overstepped. That was the last thing she'd wanted. Finally, she said, "I can't go back to the United States, unfortunately."

"Neither can I," Fox said, his voice slightly strained. "But most people can't go back home, you know? Once you go so far away and build a different life for yourself, it's like that past life dies, in a way."

"I know what you mean," Brea said.

"That's the story of Thailand, though, isn't it? It's just full of expats hiding from something or someone," Fox went on.

"I guess so." Brea hadn't considered that so many people in Thailand were like her. *Was the yoga teacher lady hiding, too?* "I heard from someone from my old life today. It freaked me out."

Fox winced. "I've been there. Is this person someone you're hiding from?"

"Yep."

Fox sighed, noted she was out of beer, and grabbed another bottle. "Do you know if you're going to respond?"

"I don't see a reason to," Brea said. "Like you said, that life is dead. And you shouldn't talk to ghosts, I guess."

"Ghosts don't usually have your best interests at heart," Fox said.

"Did you answer your ghosts when they contacted you?"

Fox thought for a moment as though he wasn't sure he wanted to answer. "I answered the first one. And that was one of the biggest mistakes of my life."

"Was it a woman?"

"A past love, sure," Fox replied. "She thought we could try again. I was living in Ko Samui at the time, and she came out there to live with me. At first, it was rainbows and gumdrops, but not long afterward, it became clear that we'd become very different people. It was devastating, too, because I'd completely upheld that relationship as one of the best of my life in the past. But by the time our second round of the relationship was over here in Thailand, we hated each other."

Fox's voice was very somber, dark. Brea recognized the tremendous pain in his eyes.

"Is your ghost a man who got away?" Fox asked after a dramatic pause.

Brea shook her head. "She used to be my best friend. We met when we were four years old and went through life together. We lived together in college, then went on to work for the same company in New York City before returning home together. She was the maid of honor at my wedding."

"When was the last time you saw her?"

"The year 2000," Brea replied.

Fox shook his head. "Is she feeling nostalgic? Is that why she reached out?"

"No," Brea breathed. "She's angry. She's so, so angry. And I'll never be able to talk her down."

"Want my advice?"

"Okay."

"Delete the message," Fox said. "Block her if you can. Don't let yourself get distracted by the past again. I mean, look around you." He swept his hand through the air to show off the turquoise waters, the blissful beaches, and the swaying palm trees. "You live in paradise. Why would you want to be anywhere else?"

Not long after, Brea took her motorbike back home, returned her neighbor's plate, and ate a mango, standing at her kitchen window, staring out yet unable to comprehend what she saw. When she finished the mango, she deleted Oriana's message— and considered blocking her. But for some reason, she couldn't bring herself to. It felt too drastic.

Chapter Four

B y the time Oriana and Meghan's four-day trip to New York City came to an end, Oriana had secured three art deals, met with five clients, attended two swanky parties— and nearly lost her mind with worry. Behind the wheel of her convertible, her head thrummed with anxiety as Meghan clicked through radio stations, looking for songs they'd previously loved as younger versions of themselves.

"This one's great," Meghan said, pumping her fist through the air as a late eighties hit came on. "Oh gosh. This reminds me of that terrible blazer I always stole from you. The one with the shoulder pads?"

Oriana tried to smile, remembering the magenta and blue blazer, which she'd caught Meghan wearing at a high school party. Oriana had taken her aside and told her she was too young for that beer and certainly too young for her blazer— and Meghan had burst into tears. Immediately afterward, Oriana had recognized her cruelty, gotten her little sister a glass of water, and driven her to a diner, where they'd eaten burgers, played songs on the jukebox, and gossiped. In retrospect, it was one of Oriana's favorite memories. They'd missed "iconic" moments at the party the night before, but neither cared.

When they boarded the ferry, Meghan and Oriana received identical text messages from their father.

> CHUCK: Hi, you two! How about dinner tonight?
>
> CHUCK: I want to hear all about your trip to the big city!

Oriana groaned inwardly, but Meghan said, "Doesn't that sound fun? Your place or mine?"

"Let me call Reese."

As Oriana and Meghan struck out from the convertible and up to the ferry's top deck, Oriana's phone rang out across the Sound. Reese answered after two rings.

"Hey, honey! You on the ferry?"

"We are." Oriana hated how down she sounded. "Dad wants to have dinner tonight."

"I know! He already let me know. We have all that burger meat in the freezer, and Alexa says we can make homemade onion rings," Reese said.

"I should have known you already had a plan," Oriana said, breathing a momentary sigh of relief.

"I got you, babe."

With the plan in place, Meghan texted her husband, daughter, Eva, and son, Theo, about dinner, and everyone agreed to come— even Eva's serious boyfriend, Finn.

"And just like that, we have a family party planned!" Meghan said happily.

Oriana gazed out across the surging waters of the Vineyard Sound, her heart in her throat and only one thing on her mind. Two days ago, she'd reached out to Brea for the first time in twenty-three years— and she hadn't responded. *Where in the world was she? Was someone threatening her, too?*

Or was Brea the one threatening Oriana? It was possible. They were strangers, now, after all. And strangers could do anything to hurt you if they wanted to. Love didn't complicate it.

Then again, Oriana knew nothing of Brea. It was entirely possible Brea was dead.

"Hey! Oriana!" Meghan's voice barely penetrated her thoughts. "We have to get back to the car now."

It was decided that en route to Oriana's place, they'd head to the retirement facility to pick up Chuck. It took ten minutes to get there from the ferry, and when they did, one of the facility workers waved to them from the front desk, recognizing them from their frequent visits. Oriana remembered a few months back when she'd come to the facility to bring her father donuts— only to be told that Roland and Grant were back there. Her half-brothers. The half-brothers who had no interest in knowing her and Meghan.

But this time, when they greeted their father, he had news on that subject.

"I saw the boys yesterday," he said as he strapped himself into the passenger seat of Oriana's car, his eyes dancing. "And they're interested in a meeting. Isn't that fantastic?"

Meghan leaned forward from the backseat. "I don't know what to say..."

Chuck bowed his head. "Girls, I've told you. The boys aren't angry with you. Their anger is directed at me — and for good reason. I broke up our family. I wronged them. And I was too much of a coward to admit it."

Oriana eyed Meghan in the rearview window. Her brain was too overloaded with other things to give this her full attention, especially because she'd heard her father say this repeatedly over the past few months.

"What if we say it's too late?" Oriana suggested, starting the engine and driving them out of the parking lot.

Chuck set his jaw, his eyes widening with surprise. Very quietly, he said, "That just doesn't sound like the woman I raised. Your mother always spoke of forgiveness and love."

Oriana blinked away tears. Ever since the incident at the hotel with the mysterious note, she'd had the strangest desire to run home to her mother— a mother who was no longer alive. She supposed that instinct never went away. Oh, how she missed her. How she yearned to lay her head on her shoulder and cry.

"We should try, at least," Meghan urged quietly. "Their children are so lovely."

"I adore them," Oriana said quickly, remembering the smiling faces of Roland and Grant's children and grandchildren. "They've made such an effort to get to know us. And I'll never forget that."

This shut everyone up for a little while.

When they reached Oriana's home, the front door burst open for Benny, who sped out onto the grass, barefoot, with his hair curly and wild after it had grown back in. The sight of her grandson filled Oriana with momentary hope, and she shut the engine off and jumped out to raise him against herself and spin around. His giggles filled her with so much love and almost made her burst into tears.

How could she protect Benny if someone was trying to destroy her?

Alexa and Reese came outside immediately afterward, Reese to kiss Oriana, and Alexa to grab the suitcases. Her arms were covered in paint from her recent painting session. She was chatty and happy, asking her aunt and Oriana about their time away.

"We almost burned the place down without you," Alexa joked to Oriana.

"Hey! Don't tell her our secrets," Reese said, swatting Alexa playfully as they entered the kitchen. Across the counter, they'd lined up the beef patties prepared for the barbecue.

Out front, another car appeared— this one belonging to Hugo, Meghan's husband. Meghan hustled to the foyer to greet him, and Oriana watched from the window as Hugo raised her up and whipped her in a circle so that her feet went out behind her. It looked like something out of a movie.

"You want me to do that to you?" Reese joked from behind her, and Oriana felt herself smile, even though she didn't want to.

"It would be nice to have a little romance around here," Oriana joked just as Reese wrapped his arms around her, closed his eyes, and kissed her lovingly. Oriana's heart swelled, even as her stomach tied itself into nervous knots.

"I love you," Reese said as their kiss broke. "I'm so glad you're home."

Out back, Hugo got to work on the burgers as the rest of Meghan's family arrived, plus Oriana's son, Joel, his wife, Lauren, and their two sons, Tyler and Peter. Oriana busied herself for a while, ensuring enough tables and chairs were outside. A sharp breeze came off the Sound, not cold enough for a full coat but certainly demanding a jacket. She hurried inside to grab blankets and extra sweatshirts just in case anyone wanted them. As she fetched them in the spare room, the one with the desk and the spare bed and several books that nobody wanted to read, she stopped short to look at the newspaper clipping that hung on the wall.

The headline of the clipping read: NEWCOMER ART DEALER MAKES KILLER, FOUR MILLION DEAL. And in the photograph beneath the headline was Oriana next to a gorgeous modern-art painting that seemed fierce, filled with passion and color. This younger version of Oriana smiled in a way that suggested she had everything figured out. It had been her first huge art deal that had set up her career. She'd known when she'd cleared the deal, that her life was about to change. And it had.

"Oriana! Where did you go?" Meghan's voice carried through the house, and Oriana hopped to it, hurrying back downstairs to deliver the blankets and sweatshirts. By the time she wiggled into a massive "Martha's Vineyard Sailing" sweatshirt, the first round of burgers and onion rings was finished. Someone put a cheeseburger on a bun for her as another person piled her plate with salad and onion rings. As she bit into the juicy burger, her muscles relaxed, and she closed her eyes at the decadent taste while the cheese melted along her tongue.

"Chuck was just telling the rest of us that Roland and Grant are up for a meeting?" Reese asked.

Oriana opened her eyes, returning to reality. "Oh. Apparently so. If they don't decide to bail at the last minute."

"They've thought long and hard about it," Chuck said, as though he were reprimanding her in her teenage years. "This has been a whirlwind of a summer for them."

Oriana nodded, unable to look her father in the eye. *What would he think when everything came to the surface? Would he think she was a fraud?*

"How are Hilary's eyes?" Alexa asked.

"All signs point to healing," Chuck said. "Although it sounds like it'll be a long road. But you know, that ex-boyfriend of hers decided to move to Nantucket to be with her and his daughter?"

"What! The one who left all those years ago?" Meghan asked.

"The very same," Chuck said. "Apparently, he wised up the minute he realized how short life can be."

"Too bad he missed his daughter growing up..." Reese sighed.

Oriana eyed her husband, her wonderful protector and best friend, and her heart thumped with the memory of how their love had grown over the years and how powerful it was. In all those years, Oriana had never considered telling Reese the truth about what she'd done. She hadn't wanted to see the disappointment in his eyes. She hadn't wanted him to share that secret.

She hadn't wanted him to know that she had been willing to do anything to succeed.

Long after her extended family left that evening,

Oriana was in the kitchen, washing the dishes and struggling to get herself to think about anything else, when the doorbell rang. A shiver ran up and down her spine.

"I'll get it!" Alexa called as she raced through the kitchen and into the foyer. After she opened the door, she called out, "It's for you, Mom! A letter?"

Oriana closed her eyes, frozen with fear. The water continued to rain down from the faucet. They'd found her. They weren't willing to let her rest.

"Bring it here, please," Oriana said, her voice cracking. She turned off the water and dried her hands as Alexa flounced in, passing the envelope off to her.

"It must be from a neighbor or something?" Alexa suggested as she opened the fridge to grab a can of La Croix. "Since it just has your name on it. Maybe a birthday invitation?"

"Probably," Oriana said, placing the envelope to the side.

Alexa eyed her mother curiously. "Aren't you going to open it?"

"Later."

"I want to know who it's from!"

Oriana swallowed the lump in her throat and shook her head. "I'm not worried about it, honey." The worst thing in the world was getting her daughter involved in this.

Alexa's nose twitched with annoyance, but then, she shrugged and spun back toward her bedroom. "All right. Good night, Mom."

"Good night, honey."

Immediately after Alexa reached the second floor, Oriana grabbed the envelope and fled to the bathroom. With the door locked behind her, she tore open the envelope, her fingers shaking. There, in the same font, were the words:

If you don't cough up three million by the end of September, I'll reveal everything.

I'll be in touch.

Chapter Five

September 1998

New York City in September was a revelation. After a long, hot summer stuck in her crummy apartment, Brea felt fresh and alive, zipping through Manhattan in a second-hand dress that had originally cost much more than her rent, en route to Oriana's apartment. Oriana had called her over to tell her "some news." And Brea had a hunch she already knew what it was.

Just before Brea hit Oriana's street, she turned left toward a pay phone, where she pushed quarters into the machine and called her love, her fiancé, Kenny. Kenny answered on the third ring, sounding groggy.

"Hello?"

"Hi, baby!" Brea's voice was high-pitched and eager. "I wanted to tell you I left work early to go to Oriana's. I might be home late."

"Thanks for letting me know, honey. Does Oriana have news yet?"

"I think she does." Brea did a little happy dance in front of the pay phone, and several people on the sidewalk gave her weird, curious looks.

"Ah, baby. I'm so happy for you. It's actually working out!"

Brea closed her eyes, her head swirling. "You have work later, right?"

"I'll be home around one, I think," Kenny replied, speaking of his job at a local restaurant, where he slaved behind a stovetop and routinely came home with oil burns on his arms. Brea frequently felt guilty for dragging the both of them from Martha's Vineyard, especially when things hadn't worked out for her. But now, with Oriana's call, she felt on the brink of something.

"Maybe we can finally start looking for a new place," Brea suggested, unable to contain her enthusiasm.

Kenny laughed gently. "Let's not get ahead of ourselves. This crummy apartment suits us just fine, for now."

Brea winced, remembering the gorgeous little house they'd shared in Martha's Vineyard, where they'd been able to walk just ten minutes to get to the beach. But she'd promised the minute her career found its footing in New York City, she and Kenny would return to Martha's Vineyard to marry and start their family. They'd both seen how chaotic Oriana's life with two babies in the city was, and they'd decided to wait a bit longer, especially because they didn't have the money to raise them comfortably.

"I love you, Kenny," Brea said, her voice catching. She thought she would remember this moment as the last time she viewed herself a struggling young woman trying to find her way and make ends meet. Very soon, she would be on her way up in the world. She just knew it.

"I love you, too."

Brea reached Oriana's apartment building ten minutes later. There, Oriana buzzed her up, and Brea leaped into the elevator, always overwhelmed with how much nicer Oriana's apartment building was. But Oriana was a real talent in the art dealing world. Last year, she'd nabbed an apprenticeship with the great Larry Gagosian, which set her up for a whirlwind of art dealings, contacts with exclusive parties, and a window into the art world that most others considered "out of reach." Although Brea ached with jealousy, Oriana had promised to give her a leg-up in the industry the minute she could.

And now that Oriana's apprenticeship was finished, it was time.

Oriana's door was cracked just a bit, and Oriana's children's cries came through the hallway. Alexa was just a baby, and Joel was two, which meant their house wasn't popular with the neighbors— and Oriana hardly got any sleep. Still, when Oriana opened the door wider to greet Brea, she smiled beautifully and propped little Alexa against her chest, a portrait of motherly health.

"Hi, Brea! I'm so glad you could come on such short notice."

For a moment, Brea was petrified that Oriana had asked her over to help her with childcare rather than help her career, especially when Joel started sobbing upon Brea's entry, and Brea picked him up and calmed him down.

"He loves you to bits," Oriana said as she stepped into the kitchen to make a bottle for Alexa.

"Where's Reese?" Brea asked.

"He's on his way back from the store. I couldn't

believe it, but we ran out of diapers. When he gets back, we're going out. Okay?"

Brea breathed a sigh of relief. Although she adored children, she wasn't used to their cries and had no idea how Oriana juggled everything at once. She supposed the higher paycheck did wonders.

"How's Reese's new job going?" Brea asked.

"He likes it," Oriana said as she sat to feed Alexa. "He's a computer whizz in all things. I swear, I don't know how his brain works half the time."

Brea smiled. She'd watched Oriana fall in love in high school alongside her and Kenny. The four of them had been forever friends, the sort with permanent Friday-night double-date plans. Kenny and Reese were almost like brothers in that way, frequently helping one another out. Still, Kenny didn't have Reese's computer skills and had gone to cooking school, which, for now, had landed him this messy job. It would get better soon. It had to.

"And how's Kenny's job?"

"He hates it," Brea said with a shrug.

"Oh no. I can't imagine how hard it is to work in a kitchen," Oriana said. "But hey. I think today might change everything for you guys."

"I can hardly wait."

Reese returned home ten minutes later with bags under his eyes from little sleep, but he smiled at his children and Brea, his long-time friend.

"I retrieved the diapers!" he called.

"God bless my husband," Oriana said as she walked Alexa back to the nursery to put her in her crib.

Minutes later, Brea and Oriana burst from her apartment, hurried for the elevator, and dropped to the ground floor. As they walked into the vibrant sunlight of the late-September afternoon, Oriana breathed a sigh of relief.

"I'm free! For now." She laughed and wrapped her arm around Brea's shoulder, tucking her close. "Brea, I can't begin to tell you how happy I am right now."

Brea thrummed with anticipation. Oh, how she needed Oriana to tell her something good! Something that would elevate her life! Something that meant she and Kenny could stop eating packages of ramen for dinner!

"I'm out on my own," Oriana announced, "and I'm bringing you on as my apprentice, if you accept. That means you'll get the same salary I've had the past year, plus all the perks. At the end of this year, I imagine you'll have a similar portfolio as me, plus your clients. And maybe, just maybe, that means we'll be able to head back to Martha's Vineyard and get the heck out of this dirty city."

Brea stopped short on the sidewalk, too overwhelmed to walk. Oriana spun around, surprised, then laughed at Brea's expression, which probably echoed shock and awe.

"You're kidding." Brea looked at her expectantly.

"Why would I kid about something like that?" Oriana said. "I told you, Brea. It's me and you till the end. Right?"

Brea rose and threw her arms around Oriana, thinking about the wonder of the next few months. About how she and Kenny would be able to find another apartment, eat better food, and maybe get some sleep. Maybe, even before they returned to Martha's Vineyard, they could get pregnant. Oh, she was filled with a longing she could hardly name.

"But tonight, your apprenticeship begins," Oriana said. "If you accept it?"

"What? Of course! Of course." Brea laughed at herself. "I mean, come on. This is exactly what I want!"

"Great. We're off to see a painting!" Oriana pointed forward, then added, "One that I want to sell for four million dollars."

It was difficult for Brea to imagine anything on a canvas costing four million dollars, especially because her apartment— a place that housed her and kept her alive — cost much less than that.

"What makes it so special?" Brea asked.

"You just have to see it for yourself," Oriana said. "I think you'll understand the magic."

The four-million-dollar painting was held in a locked studio space in Greenwich Village, not far from Oriana's apartment. Oriana used three different keys in four different locks to open the door, then led Brea into an white-walled studio that was empty, save for a single painting that hung on the far wall.

The painting was very modern— slashes of green and blue that seemed to create a sort-of face, although Brea wasn't sure. In college, she'd studied art on her quest to be either an artist or an art dealer, whatever happened first, but she'd never been able to wrap her mind around most modern art. Certainly, the painting before her seemed important in some way, but that was probably because it was the only painting hanging in the entire gallery space, protected by four locks.

It all seemed like a weird game with rules she didn't understand. But that's what made it exciting, she supposed.

"What do you think?" Oriana asked, side-eyeing her.

"It's really something," Brea lied, stepping away from Oriana to take the painting in from another angle.

"Isn't it? I met the artist at Larry's party last weekend, and he floored me when he explained the concept."

Brea raised her eyebrows, stopping herself from asking what the "concept" was. *Was it "splashes of color that sort of become a face"? Or was it something else? If Brea didn't "get" this painting, did that mean she wouldn't be a good art dealer?*

"Anyway, someone's coming by in about ten minutes to see it," Oriana said.

"Oh! Wow. Should I still be here? Or should I leave?"

"You're my apprentice now. I want you here to see how it all goes down." Oriana lowered her voice to add, "And, to tell you the truth, I'm a bit nervous."

Brea found this difficult to believe. Although she'd known Oriana since age four, she'd hardly ever seen her sweat. She'd always seemed so sure of herself, confident and able to demand what she wanted from the world. By contrast, Brea had always been quieter, less sure of herself and her voice. Still, Brea had always been the better artist — something Oriana had always said proudly. "Brea is a magnificent painter. Maybe one day, I'll get to deal her art instead."

But the fact of the matter was, Brea needed cash now. And this was a window into the art world, one she needed.

Not long afterward, a doorbell rang, and Oriana went to fetch the first potential buyer, a woman in her fifties who had a fit when Oriana said she couldn't smoke cigarettes in the gallery space.

"Who do you think you are?" the woman demanded of Oriana as Oriana apologized and said they weren't her rules.

41

"And besides," Oriana said kindly, "we want to take care of the art above all things."

With a sigh, the woman threw her cigarette down the stairwell, then entered the gallery, evoking a sense of sophistication and meanness, clear signs of serious wealth. When she saw the painting for the first time, she cupped her chin and tilted her head, looking at it with eagle eyes.

"Has Barney called you about it?" she demanded.

"He has," Oriana said with a nod.

The woman harrumphed. "I can't imagine he'd offer more than two million."

"He offered three."

The woman didn't look happy about that in the slightest. As she stepped away from the painting, Oriana spoke about the artist and his work at length, using words that made little sense to Brea but seemed to speak to the wealthy woman's sense of the world. *Had she ever created art before? Or had the words fallen from the sky— seemingly meaningless unless you owned many millions of dollars?*

After this first client left, several more came. Brea watched Oriana in her element, sweet-talking the clients about the artwork, about how in demand it was. Each time she discussed other buyers, the new clients tilted their heads like eager golden retrievers. At the end of each meeting, Oriana gave them a time limit, requiring that they tell her their bid within the next two weeks. This set a fire beneath several of them. One man in a purple suit jacket demanded to buy it immediately for two and a half million, saying he could have it sent to Oriana that evening. But Oriana knew better than to rush into a sale. If she bided her time, she could leech far more out of these people, more than they thought themselves possible of shelling out.

When it was just Brea and Oriana in the gallery, Oriana squealed and took Brea's hands. Brea was reminded of being out on the elementary school playground with Oriana, hand-in-hand, as a jump rope spun over them and flapped against the pavement beneath them. Each time, they'd had to jump to stay in the game.

"Isn't this exciting?" Oriana cried.

"It is," Brea agreed, trying to drum up Oriana's level of happiness.

"And pretty soon, everything I'm doing here will be second nature to you," Oriana went on. "I hardly hear myself anymore. I just say exactly what these people want to hear, and somehow, it works. It's weird, isn't it?"

"Yes, it is." Brea's smile waned.

"Let's get out of here! I want to make this official. We'll go to the office, have you sign the paperwork and write down your bank details, and then we'll go out to celebrate! How does that sound?" Oriana led Brea to the gallery door, where they stepped out and locked all four locks behind them.

Brea was caught up in Oriana's vortex, traveling a million miles per hour. Within thirty minutes, she sat at Oriana's desk, signing document after document as Oriana's coworkers passed by to congratulate her on this "big step forward."

"Oriana says you have a killer eye," another art dealer said, impressed. "And Oriana doesn't say that about just anyone."

Brea's cheeks burned with embarrassment. "I can't wait to get started."

Back on the streets of Manhattan, Oriana led them to a swanky cocktail bar, where the bartender greeted her by name and led her to a corner table that was slightly raised. This way, Oriana and Brea could see all of the bar dwellers. Oriana ordered them cosmopolitans, a cocktail Brea had never had enough money for, and when they arrived, they clinked their glasses and smiled. Brea decided she could get used to this.

"I know what you're thinking," Oriana said, setting down her cosmopolitan.

"And what is that?"

"You're thinking all those people are insufferable," Oriana said.

Brea blushed again. "Was it that obvious?"

"Not to them," Oriana assured her. "They're so stuck up that they hardly perceive anyone else around them. But I've known you since we were four. So, yeah. I see how sick of them you already are. But think of it this way. If you treat these people right, do them little favors, just for a little while, you can go back to Martha's Vineyard and deal art from there. We'll do it together, forming a little business to help the rich tourists of the island decorate their beautiful and very big homes. They're going to need us!"

Brea sipped her cosmopolitan, surprised at how much she liked it; hating that, more often than not, money was a very good thing to have.

"I'm not naive enough to think I can live without money," Brea assured Oriana.

"Those people have money," Oriana reminded her. "And they're not afraid to play around with it. We just have to point the money in the right direction to help both the artists and ourselves."

"It's a brilliant plan," Brea admitted. After all, her heart had only cared about three things for most of her life: Kenny, Oriana, and art itself. It seemed that this job was a fast track to having all three in her life for good.

Chapter Six

That night, Brea got home from drinks with Oriana around ten-thirty. Because Kenny had told her he had work until one, she was surprised to find him crumpled on the floor, white as a ghost.

"Kenny!" Brea dropped to the ground, stricken, and touched his shoulder. "Baby, are you all right?"

Kenny shivered beneath her hand. "I called in sick. I don't know what's wrong."

Brea kissed Kenny's cheek gently, surprised at how clammy his skin was. "Let's get you up, baby. Let's get you to bed."

Kenny shook his head and closed his eyes. "This is the first time I've felt comfortable in a few hours. I've been vomiting. A lot."

Brea jumped up and hurried to the kitchen, where she heated water for tea and searched for anything to calm his stomach. As they'd been together for many years, Brea felt she understood Kenny's immune system almost as well as her own.

"I can go to the bodega for some Sprite?" she tried.

Kenny was quiet, and Brea panicked again, hurrying over to him to find his eyes closed. She thought he was sleeping for a moment, but then, he spoke.

"I can't keep anything down."

"Why don't you try a few crackers? And tea?"

Kenny sighed and pressed his hand against the floor to lift himself. Energized, Brea headed back to the kitchen to grab his tea and crackers, then set them up in front of him. The television was on, and it flashed an eerie green light across his face. Although the volume was very low, Brea could make out MTV music videos— Pearl Jam's "Do the Evolution" was on right now.

"Did you eat something bad? Maybe you have food poisoning?" Brea asked softly.

Kenny shrugged. "I just had spaghetti for dinner before going to work. It must have sat with me wrong."

Brea frowned, remembering she'd eaten from the same pasta sauce just that afternoon. Nothing had happened to her. *Was Kenny developing an allergy?*

Not long after Kenny tried the tea, he ran back to the bathroom to vomit again. Brea shivered with worry, standing outside the bathroom to offer support if he needed it. When he came back out, he stumbled toward the couch and sat back down again.

"Maybe we should try to go to bed," Brea suggested, thinking it improbable that Kenny had anything left in him to vomit up.

Kenny finally agreed. Brea placed a large pot beside the bed, one for emergencies. Although Kenny didn't vomit again until morning, he tossed and turned all night, his sweat bleeding through the sheets. Brea hardly slept either, which was devastating the night before her first day at work with Oriana.

The following morning, Kenny sat listlessly on the couch, watching more music videos and eating a cracker very slowly as a way to test his stomach. Brea was dressed in her fanciest work outfit, which was much cheaper than anything Oriana and her colleagues wore. When her first payday came through, she'd head to the boutiques they frequented, as she knew her clothing would dictate how clients perceived her. That was part of the game.

"I'm worried about leaving you here alone all day," Brea said.

Kenny waved his hand. "I'm fine. It's just a stomach bug or something. I guess it'll work its way out of my system in the next day or two."

Brea sighed and poured him another glass of water. "If it wasn't my first day, I would call in and stay home with you."

"That would be silly," Kenny told her.

Brea rolled her eyes and stepped toward Kenny to kiss him on the forehead, then the lips. His skin remained so clammy and cold.

"I love you, Kenny," she told him. "The number for the office is on the fridge. Call me if you need anything, and I'll come home right away."

"You don't need to worry about me," Kenny assured her. "I'll be fine."

But over the next several days, Kenny did not get better. The vomiting came in fits and starts, and he lost a great deal of weight very quickly. On day three of his illness, Kenny's boss from the restaurant called and fired him, saying that Kenny didn't care about his position anyway. Brea begged him to reconsider, saying that

Kenny was very ill, but the restaurant owner coughed and hung up.

"I think we should go to the doctor," Brea told him, crossing her arms over her chest.

Kenny waved his hand. "If it doesn't clear up in the next two days, we can go."

"You promise?"

Kenny nodded. "You're going to be late for work. Come on. Don't mess up your big gig on my account."

Brea felt wordless. After she kissed Kenny goodbye and jumped into the subway to head to the office, she allowed herself a few minutes to weep into her hands. Never had she seen Kenny so sick! Of course, Kenny was bullheaded and trying his hardest not to appear as sick as he was. But Brea sensed something horrible was about to happen.

When Brea arrived at the office, Oriana rushed past her, her eyes panicked. "We need to go, Brea! Right now!"

Brea was exhausted. She'd hardly slept since Kenny's illness had begun, and the world was blurry around the edges and nonsensical. As quickly as she could, she jumped after Oriana, sitting in a cab that took them back to the gallery space in which the four-million-dollar painting was hung, expectant.

"Another client wants to see it," Oriana explained hurriedly. "Before he flies back to Tokyo this afternoon."

As they waited for the client, Oriana glanced at Brea, then furrowed her brow. "Brea, are you all right?"

Brea stuttered. "Yes? Why?"

Oriana leafed through her purse to find a small package of Kleenex. "Your makeup ran a little under your eyes."

Katie Winters

Brea took a tissue and attempted to mop herself up, feeling shaken.

"Were you crying?" Oriana asked, her business voice melting away to show the true friendship and love beneath.

"Oh, no. Nothing like that," Brea lied.

She wasn't sure why she didn't want to tell Oriana about Kenny's illness. She supposed she didn't want Oriana to send her home, thus pushing back her career even longer. She and Kenny needed the money above nearly everything else. Plus, she didn't want to verbalize her fears, which meant they were real and couldn't be ignored.

Right now, Brea could continue pretending that everything was mostly normal and that Kenny had a stomach bug.

"Is everything all right at home?" Oriana pushed it.

"Everything is great," Brea assured her. "Kenny's so happy that I have this promotion. And he's going to look for a better job— one he doesn't hate so much."

Oriana smiled. "That's wonderful news, Brea."

The doorbell rang, and Oriana righted her face and walked purposefully toward the door. "You ready?"

"Of course," Brea lied, matching her smile to Oriana's. "Let's do it."

But all the while, as Brea stood off to the side and Oriana performed her song and dance number, illustrating how much this painting was desired and truly worth, Brea felt her insides melting. *How could anything this ugly be worth four million dollars? How could Kenny be this sick?*

Nothing was making any sense.

But when Oriana turned to her and asked, "What was

50

it the woman who viewed the painting yesterday afternoon said?"

"She said it was an incendiary force," Brea said. "When she looked at it, her soul burst like fireworks."

The client nodded, his eyes shimmering with want. Brea wondered what it was like to want something so meaningless. Then again, she supposed a talent amongst humans was their ability to find meaning in almost anything— even modern art.

Chapter Seven

Present Day

Oriana had never contacted a private investigator before. It felt strange to Google "private investigators around Martha's Vineyard" and far stranger to read that there were so many. Apparently, people were a lot nosier than she thought.

To her tremendous surprise, Reese walked up behind her and saw her Google search.

"Private detectives? Why are you googling that?" Reese laughed and kissed her gently on the back of the neck.

Oriana closed her computer swiftly and laughed, the sound jangling in her ears. "I was, um. Thinking about writing a book."

Reese leaned against the counter and poured himself a cup of coffee. His hair was mussed from sleep, and his glasses were slightly crooked. Oriana thought this was how she loved him most: groggy, slightly messy, just opening himself up to the day.

"A book, huh? A crime thriller?"

"Yeah. Something like that," Oriana said. "All I've done the past twenty-six years is talk about other people's art. And because I can barely hold a pencil to a piece of paper, I thought I might try out the written art instead."

Reese's eyes sparkled with electricity. "That's incredible, honey. So, you want to interview a private detective and ask about their careers? What they've seen?"

"What their process is, I guess," Oriana lied. "I know they can't tell me about the unique details of each case, but I'd like to know how their instincts around certain facts work."

"Fascinating," Reese said. "Phew, you've never made app development look so boring."

Oriana laughed. "You love it."

Reese did love his job as an app developer, something he'd fallen into later in life when apps had begun to boom. Tech companies approached him with new ideas for apps or apps that supported their already-flourishing companies, grateful for his sharp approach to technology. The apps he'd often coded appeared in the top ten downloaded apps on both Apple and Android, which made Oriana beam with pride.

Eventually, Reese retreated upstairs to work in his office, which left Oriana alone in the kitchen, shivering with fear. Before she could convince herself otherwise, she pulled up the profile of one of the top-rated private detectives in the area: a man named Baxter Drury. But after extensive reading on his website, Oriana sensed something off about this guy— and eventually learned that he almost exclusively worked for big companies, tracking down people who'd wronged those companies. It was all based on profits.

Oriana's story was far more complicated than that.

After another hour of research, during which Alexa and Benny hurried in and out of the kitchen to fetch drinks and snacks between play sessions upstairs, Oriana read about a private detective who'd been hired to come to Martha's Vineyard last spring. Originally from California, Rita had come to the island to look for Mandy Dolores, a young woman who'd gone missing mid-spring. Through extensive research and the assistance of Steven and Isabella Montgomery, Rita had been instrumental in cracking the case and getting Mandy Dolores home safe.

A Martha's Vineyard resident to her core, Oriana had known Steve Montgomery her entire life. It was nothing to call up his auto shop and see if he could connect her personally with Rita.

Steve answered the phone at the auto shop after the second ring. "Afternoon," he said. "How can I help you?"

Was it already afternoon? Oriana glanced at the clock to find that it was nearly one o'clock. Her panic had destroyed her ability to perceive the passage of time.

"Afternoon, Steve!" Oriana's voice was overly bright. "It's Oriana Coleman."

"Hello, Oriana. I haven't seen you around lately. I guess it must be about time for a car check-up. How's that beauty of yours?"

Oriana realized Steve was right, that she hadn't taken her car in for quite some time. This was yet another thing to add to her very-long to-do list.

"I'm calling about something else," Oriana said. "It's slightly discrete."

"Whatever it is, you know I can keep a secret."

Oriana smiled to herself, remembering how, a long time ago, she'd had a minor crush on Steve before she'd decided to go steady with Reese. They'd been children back then.

"I need to hire a private detective," Oriana went on. "And I've just read something about you knowing one?"

Steve's voice brightened. "Rita. Yep. She's back on the Vineyard right now, actually."

"Oh? Working a case?"

"Just to visit," Steve said sheepishly, suggesting Rita was there to visit Steve and no one else. Because Steve had lost his lovely wife, Laura, just about a year ago, it brightened Oriana to know that Steve was opening himself up to new experiences. She wasn't sure she would have had the same strength regarding Reese.

Oh, but she didn't want to think about that.

"I wonder if I could meet with her?" Oriana asked. "I need to ask her a few questions. Again, I need this to be kept under wraps, Steve."

"Absolutely," Steve assured her. "I'll give her your contact information."

"Thank you so much," Oriana said, breathing a sigh of relief. She wasn't sure why, but involving a Montgomery family member calmed her considerably.

Because Rita was on a Vineyard vacation, she told Oriana she could meet at any time. Because Oriana wanted the utmost secrecy, she suggested they meet at a secluded beach on the other side of the island, where whoever was sending her these strange notes couldn't overhear them. Rita didn't seem surprised at the request. Oriana imagined she'd received much stranger ones over the years.

Oriana drove to the beach the following morning, explaining to Reese that she needed to run errands. She parked and gripped the steering wheel with white fingers, trying to tell herself everything would be all right. She would find a way through this, just as she had everything else.

A black car pulled up beside her a few minutes later. In the front seat was a tiny woman with a black bob. Jittery, Oriana leaped from her car and entered Rita's, sitting in the passenger seat and cupping her elbows. Rita's smile was assuring, and she had a beautiful tan, probably from hours out on the sailboat with Steve.

"Hi," Rita said. "My name is Rita. It's a pleasure to meet you."

"You, too." Oriana hated how nervous she sounded. "I'm Oriana, obviously. And, gosh. I'm just so glad to meet you."

Rita frowned, sensing the gravity of the situation. "What happened, Oriana? Whatever it is, I'll do the best I can to figure this out for you."

Oriana closed her eyes, her head spinning. "I need you to find my old best friend." After a long pause, Oriana said, "Do you want to write this down?"

But Rita shook her head. "It's better that I just remember everything, just in case. Steve mentioned this was a very delicate matter."

"It is," Oriana said. "I mean, my career is on the line. I'll be made a laughingstock." She paused, licked her lips, then added quickly, "I know that is nothing compared to some of your cases. The Mandy Dolores case was especially heinous."

"It's important not to compare cases," Rita told her. "I don't think about my past cases as I handled new ones. They're all unique."

Oriana exhaled all the air from her lungs.

"Tell me about this friend of yours," Rita went on.

"Her name is Brea Larkin," Oriana said. "She was raised here on Martha's Vineyard, just like me and Steve. We became best friends when we were four, and after that, we were inseparable until she went away."

Rita nodded. "And what year was that?"

"The year 2000."

"And you've had no contact with her since then?" Rita asked.

"No. I heard that she went to Argentina. But I don't know if she stayed there. Twenty-three years is a long time to stay in Argentina."

"True," Rita said. "What was her reason for leaving the country?"

Oriana stalled. This was exactly what she didn't want to reveal to anyone, even the private detective. "It's a long story," she said. "And one I don't want to get into."

"Okay," Rita said.

"I don't think it matters why she left," Oriana continued. "Just where she ended up. You see, I need to speak to her before the end of the month."

"There's a time limit?"

"There is," Oriana said simply. If she didn't get to the bottom of this, she would be forced to pay three million dollars – but she didn't want to get into that, either.

"Was Brea living on the island before she left? Or elsewhere?" Rita asked.

"We were in New York City for a while," Oriana explained, "until our careers took off, and we decided to move back here. I had two young children, and she wanted to start a family."

"Did she start one?"

Oriana shook her head, her heart spiking with pain.

"Any chance she left records in Oaks Bluff about where she was off to next?" Rita asked.

"I sincerely doubt it," Oriana said.

Silence hung heavily in the car. Oriana feared Rita was on the brink of telling her how impossible this case sounded. It certainly sounded like a shot in the dark to find Brea in the big, open world.

"I'll do what I can," Rita said.

"She lived on Witchwood Avenue," Oriana sputtered. "Before she left, I mean. The address was 6715."

"That's helpful," Rita offered, although Oriana wasn't sure it was. "Thank you."

"And I'll pay you handsomely," Oriana assured her. "Whatever your rate is."

"I can send that information over later," Rita said. "Right now, I'll get started on this and be in touch when I know something more."

It was clear their meeting was over. Oriana thanked Rita again, shook her hand, and quickly transferred cars. Before she could start her engine, Rita was off, speeding down the road with an intensity that seemed fitting for a private detective. Oriana had a strange taste in her mouth. She wasn't sure this was entirely right. Still, it seemed like the only way.

After all, she didn't have three million sitting around, unlike the clients she'd worked with the previous few decades. All her money was tied up, reserved for a retirement that, she and Reese hoped, would be comfortable and full of love. Hadn't Oriana worked hard enough for that, despite everything that had happened?

Could one mistake destroy her life forever?

Back home, Oriana parked in the front driveway and got out to find Alexa, Benny, and Reese in the backyard with their next-door neighbor, Alan, and his new girl-friend, Nora. Nora and Alan had been working hard in the garden all morning, and their knees were stiff with dried soil. Reese poured them each a glass of lemonade, laughing happily at a story Alan told about a bee colony he'd discovered in Northern Macedonia, one that had nearly attacked him. "I had to run away screaming!"

It was difficult for Oriana to feel a part of this community, but she tried her best to smile normally, to ask questions.

Eventually, Alexa explained that Chuck had called earlier that day to ask if Oriana and Meghan were up for a family dinner at Roland's house on Nantucket. This information caught Oriana off-guard.

"Really? They actually want to meet?" Oriana was flabbergasted.

"I guess so," Alexa said.

"It took them long enough," Nora said, as she was privy to the goings-on of the Coleman family and how prideful they often were.

"Are you up for that?" Reese asked Oriana, whose thoughts had splintered into a million directions. On the one hand, she felt lost and anxious, praying that Rita would find Brea before it was too late. On the other, she was terrified to meet her half-brothers for the first time in the flesh.

"I guess I'd better be," Oriana said, reaching to squeeze Reese's hand. At least for a moment, his touch electrified her and gave her strength to keep going, even as her stomach twisted with emotion. She felt sure she was about to float off the ground.

Chapter Eight

The Coleman family dinner was held that Saturday evening at seven p.m. Prior to departing for the docks, where Sam's boyfriend, Derek, was picking them up to bring them to Nantucket, Oriana and Meghan were hard at work in Oriana's bedroom, trying to find something to wear. Despite the past week's stress, Oriana was surprised to find that she and Meghan were frequently laughing, trying on skirts, dresses, and blouses, and gossiping about how the night would go. They were the first non-anxious minutes since her trip to New York. Oriana counted her blessings for them.

"I think the red sweater with the corduroy skirt looks amazing," Oriana said, eyeing Meghan as she twisted to and fro in the mirror.

Meghan blushed. "It's silly, isn't it? That we want to dress up to meet our brothers for the first time?"

"Not at all. I think it would be sillier if we weren't nervous. I mean, these guys have been shadows in our lives forever. We've always known about them, and we've always dreamed about what they would be like. And now, we get to find out."

"What if we hate them?" Meghan said, wincing.

Oriana laughed, her heart opening. It was entirely possible that this could happen.

"If we don't like each other, I guess we'll just go back to how things were before," Oriana said. "Nobody loses here. Besides. I bet Roland's wife is a good cook, so we'll at least get a good meal out of it."

At six-fifteen, Oriana, Reese, Meghan, Hugo, and Chuck were ready and waiting at the Oak Bluffs dock, watching expectantly as Derek's boat grew closer and closer.

"Sam's on there, too!" Oriana said, grateful to see Samantha's bright blonde hair whipping in the wind.

Derek skidded the boat along the edge of the dock as Samantha leaped out to tie up the ropes. When she'd finished, she turned to hug Oriana, then Meghan, squealing out, "I can't believe this is happening!"

"I know." Oriana shook her head. "Are they nervous?"

"I think everyone is," Sam said. "But it's only natural, isn't it?"

Oriana, Meghan, Chuck, Reese, and Hugo boarded the sailboat, helping where they could or else clinging to the railing, eyes on the frothing waves beyond. The September skies above were periwinkle, punctuated with massive clouds— some of which suggested rain. Already, Chuck had translated that they would be spending the night in Nantucket, which made Oriana apprehensive. What if the night went poorly? They would have no escape.

"Mom's cooking a feast," Sam explained, smiling.

"Hilary felt well enough to be there all day with me, keeping Mom company and helping out."

"Oh! That's great. I've thought about her so much since her surgery," Meghan said.

"I've been at her place quite a bit since it happened," Sam said. "Her daughter and boyfriend, Marc, are out in San Francisco right now, tying up loose ends, and she's needed a bit more help than she'd like to admit."

"So, Marc is officially moving out?" Chuck asked.

"It looks like it," Sam said.

"And how do you feel about that?" Oriana asked. "I mean, he left her all those years ago. You must be angry."

Sam's face twisted into a near-smile. "I wanted to stay angry, you know? But then, I saw how much Marc doted on Hilary when he got back. It seems like he never fell out of love with her. He was just too young to understand how special it was."

Oriana eyed Reese, thanking her lucky stars that Reese had never taken off on her. By contrast, he'd put aside his career aspirations for her to push herself in her career. He was a one-of-a-kind guy.

When they reached Martha's Vineyard, they tied up the boat and got into Derek's and Sam's vehicles, Oriana, Reese, and Chuck in one and Meghan and Hugo in the other. As they drove out to Roland's place, which Oriana knew was called the Coleman Family House, she shivered with expectation, then eyed her father, whose face was drawn. Probably for him, coming back to Nantucket was always an emotional rollercoaster. This was where he'd been born— this was the island he'd abandoned for the love of Oriana and Meghan's mother. It was a complicated story.

When they arrived, Roland and his wife, Estelle,

stepped onto the front porch and raised their hands. It looked almost as though they were actors playing the part of a welcoming crew. Oriana stepped out of the car and smiled up at them, waving back.

"Come on in," Estelle said, her voice bright. "Grant and Katrina are here, too."

Oriana noticed that Sam and Derek hung back near their cars.

"Are you not coming in for dinner?" Oriana asked.

"We figured it would be better for just the siblings and their spouses to be together," Sam said. "If you add children, partners, and spouses to the mix, it gets chaotic."

"Next time," Meghan urged her. "We should all be together."

"With your children and grandchildren, too," Sam said.

"Yes," Meghan said, clasping her hands. "I can't wait."

Up on the porch, Oriana and Meghan approached Roland slowly. Although Oriana had seen photographs of him, and Roland's face was remarkably like their father's, he was far taller than she'd expected him to be. Unfortunately, that made her even more nervous. What had gotten into her?

"Hello, Roland," Meghan spoke first, holding her hand out for Roland's to shake. It felt like a very heavy moment.

Roland shook it, then shook Oriana's, as his cheeks reddened. Estelle, Chuck, Hugo, and Reese entered the house, trading places with Grant, who approached to stand beside Roland, peering down at their younger sisters. Oriana thought she might pass out.

"You look so alike," Oriana said finally.

"We always did," Grant offered, his voice breaking.

"You two look alike, as well," Roland said. "Hard to believe you're the same people as those little girls I saw Dad with all those years ago."

Chuck had explained that Roland had followed their father and seen him in a restaurant with Mia and two little girls. He'd understood those little girls to be his sisters.

"I guess we grew up," Meghan tried.

"I guess we all did." Roland slid his fingers through his thick, salt-and-pepper hair.

It was clear nobody knew what to say. Oriana found herself mourning all the years they'd spent apart from one another, all the while knowing that the other half of their family was on an island a few miles away. *Why hadn't she come to this house and banged down the door?*

"Everyone?" Estelle popped her head back onto the porch, perhaps sensing things had gotten awkward. "I have appetizers and a bunch of wine on the table. Help yourself, okay?"

"Wine sounds great," Meghan said, stepping around Roland and Grant. Oriana followed close on her heels, trying to stamp out her instinct to take her little sister's hand.

On the back porch, Oriana took in their splendid view of the rolling green hills aligned with a wide stretch of sparkling white beach. Although her place with Reese on Martha's Vineyard was like heaven on earth to her, she understood that Roland's house was infinitely more expensive and ornate. Probably, he'd worked hard for it. That, and he'd taken Chuck's money to keep quiet about Chuck's affair.

Oriana decided it was better not to think about that, especially not right now.

Estelle had made a number of appetizers: stuffed mushrooms, bruschetta, salmon puffs, spinach pastries, and tiny seasoned pieces of chicken. Oriana sat between Meghan and Reese, her protectors, and watched as Roland poured her a glass of Primitivo.

"Shall we make a toast?" Estelle suggested when everyone had been served wine.

"I don't see why not," Meghan said.

Oriana lifted her wine, watching her hand quiver slightly, giving away her nerves. To add horror to it all, she wondered if her spy could see her now, if he knew about her second family, about their rejection of her until now. She didn't like to think of this horrible person out there, knowing such intimate details about her.

"It's been a long time coming," Grant said quietly, making eye contact with Oriana and Meghan. "And that's been our fault."

"But we're here now," Meghan said. "Which is all that matters."

Oriana wasn't so sure she was fully ready to forgive. Then again, there was an open kindness and honesty in both of their eyes, one that reminded her of her father when she'd been a girl. This nostalgia was so sharp that it pained her.

"Oriana," Roland began, "I'm not ashamed to admit that I've followed your career over the years."

Oriana's eyes widened with surprise. "Have you?"

"Of course. Your name pops up frequently in my social circles, especially when I travel for work," Roland said. "People seem to respect your artistic eye. An associate of mine out in LA waited over a year before you had time to come out there and advise him on the pieces you could sell him for his space."

"You're talking about Gregor Balkin?" Oriana remembered the Bulgarian man who'd had a fit when she couldn't come out to California immediately.

"The very same. He's a trip, isn't he?" Roland said.

Oriana laughed. "He's certainly a personality. I don't know if it's a personality I like, but..."

Roland burst out, his eyes alight. "That's very well put. I don't know if I would have been quite as kind in my description."

Oriana was surprised at how easy it was to make her seemingly serious half-brother laugh.

"You must have worked with some incredible people over the years," Estelle said.

"She has," Meghan piped in, happy to brag about Oriana. "About two weeks ago, she let me go with her to New York. She was invited to all these swanky parties and expensive apartments to rub shoulders with people in that world. I wanted nothing to do with it, obviously. It's not my thing. But Oriana just flourishes."

"It's like playing a character in a story that doesn't belong to you," Oriana suggested.

Roland nodded. "I've found that happens to me often, especially when I'm surrounded by people who can't understand Nantucket or our way of life here on these islands. City people who think their lives are so much better than mine."

"Oriana lived in the city for a while," Meghan continued to brag.

Oriana kicked Meghan under the table, trying to get her to stop that.

"Did you? I always thought that seemed so dreamy," Estelle said.

"What do you do, Estelle?" Oriana asked, wanting to take the conversation topic away from her and her career — the career that was probably out the window soon if Rita didn't track down Brea.

"Oh, it's not important," Estelle said, waving her hand.

"She's a very popular romance writer," Roland bragged, touching his wife's shoulder. "I don't know why you never want to talk about it."

But Oriana understood. As women, it was much easier to shove aside your accomplishments, if only so that nobody felt nervous or that you were bragging. In some people's eyes, there was nothing worse than a woman talking about how great she was doing. Oriana knew this was a problem with society, but not one they could solve today.

Still, it seemed Roland was willing to uphold his wife's accomplishments. And Oriana had to respect that.

After that, their conversation found solid ground, with Oriana, Meghan, Grant, and Roland asking questions about one another's children, their careers, and the decades of their lives they'd collectively missed. Never was there an air of accusation, only of regret. More wine was poured while salmon and trout were served, as was an astonishing raspberry dessert that knocked Oriana's socks off. As they showered Estelle with compliments, Estelle blushed the color of the raspberries, and Oriana reached for her wine to give another toast. For the first time in ages, her mind wasn't wasted on her fears surrounding her blackmailer. She was safe, surrounded by family members.

And a part of her knew, too, that if she told them what she'd done— they wouldn't hate her. Maybe they wouldn't fully understand why she'd done it. But they wouldn't hate her.

"I can't thank you enough for this evening," Oriana said with her glass raised. "Here's to many more nights, just like this. Surrounded by the people I love."

Chapter Nine

1998

One week after Kenny got sick, Brea finally convinced him to go to the doctor. Unfortunately, the appointment fell at the worst possible time— in the middle of several meetings Brea had to attend with Oriana.

Kenny also didn't want to tell Oriana about the doctor's appointment. He urged Brea to go to the meetings if only to keep up the ruse that nothing was wrong.

"And the doctor will probably just tell me I drank too many beers or something!" Kenny said, still white as a sheet as he sat up in bed, skinnier than ever.

Brea was stricken with worry. She curled up beside him, her arm slung over the flat of his stomach, her mind whirring. Neither of them had had a full night's sleep since Kenny's illness had begun, which had meant for killer workdays for Brea, during which she'd had to pretend she was A-okay for Oriana. If she slagged for just a second, she knew Oriana's coworkers and bosses would question why Oriana had hired Brea instead of someone far more connected and qualified. Brea couldn't have that.

Brea showered in cold water and changed into a trendy suit jacket and black dress that Oriana had lent her. "You can borrow stuff until your first check comes in," she'd said, suggesting that she'd been embarrassed about Brea's clothes since she'd started, which might have bothered Brea more, had she not been so deathly worried for Kenny's life.

"You should take a taxi to the doctor's office," Brea said as she adjusted her hair in the mirror, prepared to leave. "There's cash on the counter."

Kenny groaned. "We can't afford taxis, Brea."

Brea turned around and gave him a look that meant business. After a dramatic pause, Kenny folded his lips and shrugged. "All right. I'll take a taxi."

"Good." Brea ground her teeth together and stared at him, outraged with herself for not making time to go to his doctor's appointment. In fact, she wouldn't miss it. How could she? This was the man she loved, the one she wanted to move through time with. But just as she opened her mouth to tell him so, Kenny interrupted her.

"You're going to work. We can't both lose our jobs," Kenny insisted. "And you know how weird Oriana gets when someone is sick. She'll make a big show of it. She won't leave me alone. The entire apartment will be filled with casseroles that neither of us will be able to eat."

Brea laughed gently, although she wasn't sure she found anything funny right then. As she walked toward him, her heart thrumming in her chest, she remembered their first kiss at the Martha's Vineyard football field a few minutes after someone had thrown the final touchdown and the crowd had gone wild. She'd felt his heart beating through her coat, the stories of their lives braiding together, and the softness of his lips upon hers. It was as though they'd been transported through time.

But Brea had never imagined they'd be transported here to this impossibly terrible moment.

After Brea kissed Kenny goodbye, she hurried to the office to find Oriana in a state of panic.

"We have to cancel all the meetings today," she told Brea, dragging her into her office, "because Walter Billington wants to see the painting. And I know, if we play our cards right, we'll be able to sell that thing for four million. No more of this two or three million." Oriana set her jaw. "Are you ready for this? It's going to be an intense day."

Brea heard herself tell Oriana she was ready and would do whatever it took. Internally, however, she felt weaker than ever. Most of her soul was back home with Kenny, wanting to help him get ready to go to the doctor. She wanted to hold his hand as they checked him out. She wanted to hear the doctor say firsthand that Kenny would be all right.

In the cab on the way to the gallery space, Oriana explained what she knew of Walter Billington.

"He's one of the richest entrepreneurs in Manhattan, for sure," she began. "His mother is a French heiress, and his father is an American businessman, and he inherited her wit and charm and his father's business smarts. He must be about twenty years older than us. But he's married to a woman around our age. And..."

"What?" Brea demanded when Oriana went quiet.

"And he'll probably expect us to go out with him tonight," Oriana continued. "It's a part of who he is. He paints the town red, so to speak, and he likes to feel that the people he makes deals with can keep up with him."

Brea wanted to groan, scream, cry, and tell Oriana flat-out that she had to be home that night to hear what had happened with the doctor. But that moment, the taxi yanked to a halt outside the gallery, and Oriana paid the driver and bustled out. Brea could only follow her.

Walter Billington arrived fifteen minutes later than he'd said he would, which, Oriana said, wasn't too bad compared to most rich people who didn't need to treat anyone with respect. When he strode into the gallery space, Brea was struck with the feeling that she'd never seen anyone quite as handsome, that he had a European air about him with an American charm that reminded her of cowboy films. He entered alone, having told his body-guard to wait outside. Apparently, he wanted to experi-ence the artwork without anyone else's input.

And even when Oriana greeted him, Walter raised his hand and said, "Please. I go by first impressions of the piece before anything else. I don't want the art's narrative. I want to feel it myself."

Oriana nodded, closing her mouth. Walter stepped closer, crossed his arms over his chest, raised his chin, and gazed at the painting for a long time. When Brea thought he was finished with his assessment, he took a step to the right as though to take it in from another angle. Brea wanted to roll her eyes into the back of her head, but she managed to stop herself.

After probably twenty full minutes without a single word, Walter turned toward Oriana, sniffed, and said, "Okay. Tell me about the artist."

Oriana was like a very tight spring, ready to explode. Immediately, she launched into a story about the artist, who'd come from nothing and was interested in "the way people perceive the void of their lives," whatever that meant. It seemed to ring true for Walter, though. His eyes echoed how pleased he was.

"We'll go out tonight," Walter said, his eyes flickering between Oriana and Brea. "And we'll discuss the next steps. If that sounds all right with you?"

"Wonderful, Mr. Billington," Oriana said.

"Please. Call me Walter."

Oriana and Brea were wordless as Walter turned on a heel and breezed out of the gallery, back into the stairwell, where he disappeared. Oriana remained very quiet, so much so that Brea was worried she wasn't breathing.

And then, Oriana fell to her knees, her hands in fists, and cried out, "Yes!!!!!"

Brea couldn't help it. She laughed. The situation was so comical, so outside of time, that she felt she was in some kind of ridiculous film. Finally, she grabbed Oriana's hand and pulled her back to her feet, where Oriana wrapped her arms around Brea and said, "I couldn't have done that without you. I was so nervous! You were a stabilizing force."

Brea shrugged, unsure what to say.

"We have to go shopping," Oriana said. "We need to look the part of Manhattan clubbers." She then turned to her side and placed her hands on her stomach, wincing.

"You can't see it anymore," Brea answered without needing to be asked. "You lost the baby weight quickly."

"I'm sure you will too when the time comes," Oriana said, smiling graciously— pleased that she'd dropped the weight from breastfeeding and going on long walks, most of them with Brea.

"Let's not get ahead of ourselves," Brea said, trying to smile.

"Right. Shopping first. We'll welcome your babies later on."

"After we sell the painting."

"Oh, yes. After that, indeed," Oriana said, dragging Brea back toward the door.

As they shopped that afternoon, diving in and out of little Manhattan boutiques, trying on skinny dresses, having their hair styled and their makeup done, Brea allowed herself to think of them as teenagers long before "real" life had begun. She imagined the person in the next dressing room was fifteen-year-old Oriana, gossiping about her crush on Reese, which had come after a brief crush on Steve Montgomery. "I just don't think Steve likes me like that. I think he likes Laura. Which is okay because... I mean, Reese is just about the cutest guy around, isn't he?"

But each time Brea stepped from the dressing room, she was shocked to find an adult version of Oriana, wearing a cocktail dress, her makeup done to perfection. *Where had the time gone?* And oh, gosh. Kenny was probably back home from his doctor's appointment by now.

"Hey, Oriana? I'm going to call Kenny at home," Brea said as she placed three dresses back on their hangers.

"I think I saw a payphone outside," Oriana said. "You want to tell him about our victory?"

"Yeah. Exactly."

But outside, the phone rang and rang and rang until Kenny finally answered it, sounding groggy.

"Hey, honey!" Brea almost didn't recognize her voice. "How was the appointment?"

"Oh. It was fine. They're going to call me tonight with news," Kenny said.

Brea's heart sank. She'd wanted him to announce just how fine he was right now if only to ease her mind.

"Did they give any indication what it could be?" Brea asked.

"They didn't want to throw out a ton of diagnoses before they got the results back," Kenny said. "But they're rushing them."

Brea wasn't sure if needing to rush the results was necessarily a good sign. She swallowed the lump in her throat.

"How is your crazy day at work?" Kenny asked. He didn't sound angry, just tired.

"Oh. It's fine. Apparently, the client needs us to go out with him tonight to see if we're 'up to his satisfaction' as business partners. I can try to get out of it, though."

"No. Don't." Kenny sounded adamant. "All you'll do here is watch me get sick. It's..." He paused, sounding depleted. "It's honestly better to have the night to myself, baby. Because I feel so guilty when you see me like this. I can't be healthy for you right now. I'm sorry."

Brea's eyes filled with tears, and she dropped her forehead on the payphone, which was strangely sticky and cold. "I want to be with you."

Kenny was quiet, and Brea stirred with confusion. On the one hand, she understood his problem, that he saw how frightened she was and that this made him even more miserable. But on the other, didn't he want her there? Didn't she offer emotional support?

"Just come home when you're done," Kenny said. "And I'll tell you what the doctor said."

Brea stifled a sob and wiped her cheeks. She had to do

what Kenny wanted her to do right now. He was in charge, as was Oriana. Brea was like a leaf in a stormy wind.

"I love you, Kenny," Brea told him. "I love you to pieces."

"I love you, too, Monkey," he said. "Goodbye."

Just a few seconds after Brea hung up the phone, Oriana appeared on the sidewalk, carrying two cocktail dresses wrapped in protective plastic.

"I think these will work for tonight," she said. "We don't have long before we meet him for dinner. Let's go back to the office and prep."

Brea nodded, resolute. She had to make tonight work. Otherwise, it was a waste of time in literally every respect — and she just couldn't take that. She owed it to Kenny to become something. Especially now.

Chapter Ten

Dinner with Walter Billington was the fanciest Brea had ever experienced— nearly-rare steak, shrimp cocktails, buttery mashed potatoes, caviar, and martinis. The restaurant itself seemed taken from a film, with walls painted in black and servers all in black, never smiling. According to Oriana, you only got into the restaurant if you were "someone special." Otherwise, there was a three-year waiting list for reservations.

Although Brea wasn't especially impressed with wealth, she was surprised that she liked Walter Billington. As he sat with them, he spent equal time speaking with Oriana as he did with Brea, a rarity amongst the elite. When Brea told him she was just starting out in the art dealing world, he tilted his head and said, "It's because you're an artist yourself, isn't it?" And Brea blushed and said, "I guess I used to think I was."

To this, Walter placed the tip of his first finger on the table and shook his head. "You're an artist. Say it."

Brea frowned and placed her martini back on the

table. The drink had gone to her head. "What do you mean?"

"I mean, tell me you're an artist. Say it out loud."

Brea smiled, feeling foolish. "I'm an artist?"

"Say it like you mean it," Walter insisted.

Brea giggled so that her shoulders shook up and down. Beside her, Oriana nodded, urging her along. She had to do what the client wanted her to do. That was clear.

"I'm an artist," Brea said with more clarity, setting her jaw.

"Okay. I'm halfway to believing you," Walter said. "But your homework is to work on that, okay?"

"Okay," Brea said.

Throughout the entire dinner, Walter didn't bring up the painting, not once. Instead, he really got to know them — learning about Oriana's children, her husband, Reese, and Brea's fiancé, Kenny.

"The four of you were best friends in high school?" Walter looked flabbergasted.

"We were," Oriana admitted nervously.

"I think that's wonderful. Most everyone I went to high school with turned on each other or tried to use one another for wealth, or you know, married and divorced one another in horrific ways," Walter went on.

"That's terrible," Brea said.

"It is. But I never felt that any of them had compassion." Walter leaned back in his chair, impressed with them.

Oriana's eyes glinted. Brea sensed it, too. If Walter liked them, he would purchase the painting— and that meant a four-million-dollar deal. It meant Oriana proving herself, which also meant Brea proving herself. It meant colossal leaps in their careers.

But all this wild conversation and sensational food did little to alleviate Brea's fears surrounding Kenny. *Had the doctor called yet? Should she run home and learn the news? Should she call him? Or did he want her to leave him alone for one more night?*

When they reached the dance club, the bouncer waved them in immediately, recognizing Walter. As Brea followed them, her ears filled with the pulsing beat of the club music, and she found herself in a sea of partiers, all dressed in black, their hair styled, chokers on their necks. This was a far cry from the beach parties she and Oriana had frequented as high schoolers. This was terrifying.

But a few minutes later, Walter pressed a martini in her hand and said, "Let's go dance!" And Brea again followed the two of them into a smaller room, where another DJ played his tunes, his head pumping. Brea swayed back and forth as Oriana and Walter got into it, never dancing romantically but genuinely having fun with one another. By contrast, Brea felt like a little kid, dragged to the dance by her older sister. She wasn't jealous of her, per se. She just knew Oriana had skills she didn't have.

After what seemed like forever, but was probably only about a half-hour, Brea cut through the crowd and headed toward the front of the club, where a woman at the ticket booth told her she couldn't use the telephone at the club. "There's one down the road," she told her.

Brea sighed. "I can get back in after I go, right?"

The woman nodded. "Sure."

Brea dropped back into the night, shivering in the late September chill. When she reached the payphone, she

dropped quarters into it and listened as it rang and rang. When Kenny answered it, he sounded groggy, as though he'd been asleep.

"Baby! Are you sleeping?"

"What? Yeah."

It had been a while since Kenny had allowed himself to fall asleep. Brea's heart lifted. "I'm so sorry for waking you up. I just wanted to check in to see if the doctor called?"

"Oh. No. He didn't call."

"He didn't?"

"No. He must have forgotten."

Brea frowned, switching the phone from one ear to the other. "And you're feeling a little bit better?"

"Sure am," Kenny said.

Brea allowed herself to smile, if only for a moment, then told Kenny how much she loved him and that she'd be home soon.

"I told you. Enjoy your wild night," Kenny urged her.

Brea returned the phone to the cradle and hurried back to the club, rejuvenated. Maybe the doctor hadn't called because there was nothing to report. Maybe he'd decided he needed to call all those other sick people— and not Kenny. Never Kenny. He'd even found a way to sleep. God bless his heart.

Inside the club, Oriana and Walter had met a new friend. He was in his early thirties, maybe, with just as much charisma as Walter. He was dressed immaculately, and his hair was flung back in a mess that was, Brea, knew, incredibly stylish in this day and age.

"Brea! This is Nick!" Oriana called over the pumping music. "Walter knows him!"

"Hi, Nick!" Brea shook Nick's hand.

"Brea! I've heard so much about you," Nick said, although Brea wasn't sure she believed him. "Walter has fallen in love with the both of you. And do you know how picky my man is about his friends?" Nick guffawed with laughter.

Oriana and Brea exchanged smiles just as Walter returned with a platter of shots of the club's most expensive tequila. Brea accepted a glass, her head swimming with alcohol. But she knew she couldn't say no. Walter expected a show.

"To one hell of a night!" Nick said, clicking his glass against theirs.

After another round of drinking, Oriana grabbed Brea's hand, told the guys they were headed to the bathroom, and dragged her through the crowd. When they were out of their line of sight, Oriana spun around, gripped Brea's shoulders, and squealed, "We did it, Brea! He just told me on the dance floor! Four million! He's going to pay!"

Brea stuttered with surprise. It felt as though they'd just climbed an impossibly tall mountain. She flung her arms around Oriana, and they leaped up and down together, giggling.

"And I think that Nick guy is made of money, too," Oriana said as their hug broke. "He asked me to show him a few of our other pieces this week. Brea, if we keep this up, there's no way we won't be back in Martha's Vineyard, working on our own, by the end of next summer. It's happening. It's really happening."

Brea finally managed to escape the nightclub around one in the morning, when she splurged and took a taxi back home. She would remember this taxi splurge for the rest of her life.

When Brea entered the apartment, she heard Kenny again, getting sick. Her heart sank into her stomach.

"Kenny?" She hovered outside the bathroom for a moment, waiting until Kenny appeared, looking worse than ever. His skin was gray.

"Hi, baby." Kenny limped toward the couch and fell to the edge. "How was the night?"

Brea sat beside him and placed her hand on his leg. All she wanted in the world was to take his pain away.

"It was okay," Brea said. "I'm sorry you woke back up. Maybe I shouldn't have called you in the first place."

"It was okay that you called. I loved hearing your voice," Kenny assured her, his shoulders slumping.

Brea's eyes filled with tears. Something was very wrong. "Kenny, what did the doctor say?"

Kenny mumbled to himself. She could tell now that he'd been lying earlier to her— that he'd just wanted her to have a last night out before everything fell apart.

"He says I need a kidney transplant," Kenny said quietly.

Brea's eyes widened. "What? What do you mean?"

"I have an autoimmune disease. I guess I've always had it, but it's only rearing its ugly head right now," Kenny explained. "And if I don't get a new kidney..." He shrugged. "It's over."

Brea would not stand for this. "What are you talking about? Over? You're twenty-five years old!"

Kenny remained silent, staring at his feet. Brea had no idea what you were supposed to say in a situation like this. She and Kenny had only ever lived a life of romance, singing songs and running around the island of Martha's Vineyard in the sun. Their lives had never been threatened; neither had their love.

Finally, Kenny turned to look her in the eye. "I don't have insurance, Brea. So, let's get realistic about what's next, okay? It's easier if I just stare this thing in the face."

Brea's jaw dropped. "Kenny! Come on. We're going to get you that kidney."

But Kenny shook his head again and walked back to the bed. There, he collapsed and curled into a ball, shivering. Brea remained on the couch, completely shattered.

Oh, gosh. It didn't make sense. It really didn't. Brea pressed her palms hard against her eyes until she saw white spots floating in the black and traced her mind for something to do, anything that would solve this. *How could she have spent today in exquisite boutiques, eaten red meat that cost an arm and a leg, and danced in a nightclub that featured mostly celebrities who had more money than God? How could she lurk in those circles, only to come home to a fiancé without enough money to keep himself alive?*

She had to do something to keep him in the world with her, to keep them together. She just wasn't sure what.

Chapter Eleven

Present Day

Several days after meeting Roland and Grant for the first time, Oriana traveled to New York City on business— this time alone. When she breezed into the foyer of the Dominick Hotel, Meghan texted her, asking if she wanted to meet for lunch, and Oriana shivered with a feeling of loss and dread. Hadn't she told her family she was off to the city for the week? Or, with the stress from the blackmailer, had she begun to lose sight of the pieces of her life, allowing herself to abandon her sister, her dearest friend?

In the elevator, Oriana texted her sister that she'd come to New York "spontaneously" and then checked her messages from Rita, the private investigator. There was nothing new to report. Apparently, Brea had fallen off the face of the earth. *Great.*

Although Oriana had worked for herself since she'd left New York City nearly twenty-five years ago, she was still affiliated with her first company. In this place, she'd had her apprenticeship and grown into herself as an art dealer. The company's current CEO, Gretchen Garris, was a sort-of friend, a wealthy woman in the art world who took no crap and proved her worth, even though, sometimes, that meant taking down people who stood in her way. Gretchen had asked Oriana to go to dinner with her on her first night back in the city, and, due to Gretchen's power in the industry, Oriana couldn't say no.

Oriana took a short, anxious nap, then rose to shower, do her hair and makeup, and dress in black tights, a black dress, and artistic earrings that hung like baubles. In the taxi to the restaurant, she reminded herself of all the important names in the art world, plus Gretchen's husband and daughter's names. She needed to play the part of Gretchen's friend, at least for one night.

When Oriana approached Gretchen's table, Gretchen stood to her full six feet, touched Oriana's arms gently, and said, "Oh, darling. Don't you look marvelous? That island life must be healthy for you."

Oriana assumed Gretchen meant that Oriana wasn't stick-thin, like New Yorker women, and that she had a bit of meat on her bones. It was probably a backhanded compliment. Still, Oriana took it in stride, knowing she could never show weakness in front of a woman like Gretchen. Once she did, Gretchen would slowly eat her alive.

Gretchen and Oriana ordered aperitif and regarded one another: two very important women in the art world, with Gretchen in charge of some of the most sought-after dealers in the city. Oriana couldn't understand why so many of those dealers didn't want to break out on their own, although she imagined Gretchen offered a bit of safety.

"Now, before we order dinner, I'd like to get one thing out of the way," Gretchen began, folding her hands beneath her chin.

Oriana's blood pressure spiked. *What could Gretchen possibly need to tell Oriana about the art world that Oriana didn't already know? Was it possible that Gretchen knew about the blackmailer? Had she begun to tell everyone what she'd done in 1998?*

"All right," Oriana said simply, her voice wavering.

"The fact is, you've been one of the greats in this business for just about as long as anyone can remember. And people in the art world have long memories," Gretchen said.

Oriana's stomach twisted into knots. Where was she going with this?

Gretchen leaned across the table, her eyes ominous. "I've just received word that it's you this year."

Oriana remained quiet. *Her? This year? What?*

"For the award, of course," Gretchen continued. "The Brad Quinn Award in Commitment to Art. You've gone further in pushing the artistic agenda, getting names out there, and making artists rich— than nearly any other art dealer I can think of. And imagine! You've done all of that from that dinky island of yours."

Oriana was speechless. She downed the rest of her aperitif and made eye contact with the waiter, wanting to order something a little harder.

"Say you're thrilled," Gretchen ordered.

"I'm thrilled?"

Gretchen smiled. "The award ceremony is the first week of October. Make sure you wear something absolutely iconic. I have a contact at Valentino if you want that information."

Oriana needed to say something, to verbalize just how much this meant to her. After all, she'd given so much of her life to this cause. She'd believed in it the entire way, save for that one enormous mistake.

But worst of all, the first weekend of October was after the blackmailer's end date. If she didn't figure out who this was and stop it, her career would be ruined before the ceremony. Oh, gosh. She could just imagine the headlines in all the art magazines. She could just imagine their cruelty.

"I'm looking forward to celebrating you," Gretchen said icily, making Oriana question if Gretchen cared for her at all.

"It's every woman's dream," Oriana breathed, grateful as the waiter finally returned with a big glass of wine. She needed to douse her thoughts and fears with a bit of alcohol. She needed the world to go blurry for a while.

* * *

After several business meetings the following day, during which many of her clients congratulated her on her upcoming award, Oriana returned to the hotel, dressed to the nines, and headed back out into the night. She had plans to meet an old friend— and the timing couldn't have been more perfect.

Ever since they'd met in the nineties, Walter Billington had lived in a gorgeous old-world building on the Upper East Side— a place with ornate crown molding, a doorman with an elaborate uniform, and a history that included affairs, murders, spontaneous marriages, celebrities, and so much more. Because Walter had more money than he knew what to do with, he often said he liked living in the midst of so many other people's stories — as stories were free but also worth more than anything he could understand.

Walter was twenty years older than Oriana, which put him at seventy. It seemed strange for a powerful man like that to age, as though money should have allowed him to remain in his forties forever. Still, time came for everyone.

Oriana got on the elevator and went to the top, where Walter's apartment took up the entire floor. When the doors opened, Walter's wife, Priscilla, greeted Oriana with a gentle smile, took her coat, and said, "Walter's in the dining room. He's looking so forward to seeing you."

As Walter had always liked keeping his business affairs and private life separate, Oriana didn't know Priscilla very well. They had been married for as long as anyone could remember. Yet, Priscilla was often not at Walter's public appearances, and they'd rarely been photographed together. Oriana suspected Priscilla liked it that way.

"Oriana! Welcome back to the city!" Walter stood up from the dining room table and greeted her with a bear hug. Oriana suspected most billionaires didn't bear-hug (or hug at all), and it touched her.

"Thank you." Oriana blushed and sat at the table, drinking him in. He'd recently dyed his hair, and his eyes were alight and alive, just as animated as they'd been the first day she'd met him. "You look great, Walter."

"Don't flatter me," Walter ordered, just as one of his waitstaff approached to pour them both glasses of wine. "It's you I want to hear all about. How are you? How's your grandson?"

Oriana blushed at Walter's gentle nature and his

ability to remember everything. "Benny is healthy as a clam, running around the house like a monster. It's hard to believe he was ever so sick."

"I can't tell you how happy that makes me," Walter said.

Walter had been instrumental in securing the best pediatric oncologist on the east coast. It was something Oriana would never be able to thank him enough for. It had changed her life and her family's life.

In fact, Walter had changed Oriana's life in many ways over the years. The first of those ways hung just off to the left, in the hallway beside the dining room. It was there Walter kept the modern art painting she'd first sold to him in 1998— her very best deal at the time. Four million dollars. It had kickstarted her career and allowed her to return to Martha's Vineyard, just as she'd planned. As usual, Oriana tried not to look at the painting too hard. It brought back too many memories.

"I heard a rumor about an award," Walter said, his eyes shining.

Oriana blushed. "It's silly, isn't it?"

"Why would that be silly? You're a marvelous art dealer. Just look around you, Oriana. Every single piece of art in this entire apartment was something you brought to me because you understood my taste on such a unique and personal level." Walter gestured toward a sculpture on the side table, one Oriana had secured from an artist from Indonesia, along with a smaller painting on the dining room wall of an orchid from a painter from Vietnam.

"I mean, heck." Walter laughed and stood to see the painting in the hallway better. "Don't you remember the first day you showed me that painting? I came out to meet you in that gallery space, and you initially tried to charm me."

"But you told me you wanted to let the art speak for itself or something."

"Right. I did that. Can you believe how pretentious I was?" Walter chuckled. "In any case, that was one of the very first major art purchases I ever made. It felt like a big deal to me. I was asking myself what kind of collector I wanted to be. And some combination of that art, and the woman selling it, spoke to me."

Oriana's cheeks burned with embarrassment.

"But I didn't let you have that deal easily," Walter remembered. "I forced you out on the town with me if I remember correctly. You and that wonderful assistant of yours. What was her name?"

Oriana's voice was nearly stuck in her throat. "Brea."

"That's right! Brea. She was smart as a whip and very funny. What ever happened to her? Did she leave the industry?"

"She did, yes," Oriana said softly. "We lost track of each other over the years."

That was the understatement of the century.

"Well. You had the tenacity to stick around," Walter went on, "And now, look how they're rewarding you! It's completely deserved."

Walter went on to say that he was interested in two of the paintings she'd recently told him about and that they could finalize the deals as early as this week if she wanted to. This perked Oriana up for a little while, distracting her from the chaos of her mind and her fears about what would come next. Occasionally, she assessed Walter, wondering if he was picking fun at her or if he'd figured out what had happened. Maybe he was pretending to blackmail her as a joke because he'd learned the truth. That was sort of something Walter would do, she supposed. He had so much money. He didn't need three million from her.

After dinner, Walter and Oriana said goodbye with another hug, and Oriana escaped down the elevator and into the electric night of Manhattan. For a few blocks, she walked with her hands in her coat pockets, her head swirling with worries and memories. Just before she got into a cab, Meghan texted her to ask how her trip was going, and Oriana was so distracted, so lost in her mind, that she promptly forgot to write her back.

She was more selfish than she'd been in ages. But she had no idea what would happen when her world fell around her. And the worry had begun to eat away at her mind.

Chapter Twelve

Oriana hadn't heard from the blackmailer in nearly two weeks. This had left her feeling anxious, wanting to look over her shoulder constantly. With limited success, she tried breezing through life as though the bogeyman wasn't chasing after her— as though her world wasn't about to crash down around her. Everyone was very congratulatory about her upcoming award, coming out of the woodwork to write her emails and messages or call her on the phone. Reese doted on her, calling her his "multi-talented and gorgeous wife." She felt she didn't deserve any of the praise nor the love.

Still, Rita hadn't found Brea, which made Oriana lose her mind. She'd begun to question if she'd made up the entire story or if Brea still existed at all. At one time, Oriana and Brea had been so close that spending one day apart had felt like a nightmare. Now, she was petrified to ask Reese about her, to confirm she either had or hadn't existed. She imagined him saying: *"Who's Brea? What are you talking about?"* and then having her committed.

As days pressed toward that horrific end of September time limit— at which point the blackmailer would supposedly demand three million dollars, Oriana found herself working diligently, just like always. She sold three paintings to high rollers, then called several clients worldwide with information about additional works, about artists they would surely be interested in. And she played the part of a kind and compassionate grandmother and mother, frequently playing on the floor with Benny, laughing with Alexa, and cooking up grand dinners that had Alexa and Reese groaning with fullness.

"You've been running yourself ragged the past few weeks," Reese pointed out, watching her as she slid another tray of chocolate chip cookies into the oven.

Oriana clipped the door closed and wiped her hands on a kitchen towel. "You know how I get when I slow down."

Reese chuckled and kissed her, frowning gently. "Just promise me you'll take a break one of these days. Maybe we can take a drive out to the new Aquinnah Cliffside Overlook Hotel, book a room, and pretend we're on vacation."

"It does look amazing over there," Oriana admitted, trying to imagine herself falling upon a perfectly made California King bed in a suite overlooking the Sound. The image failed her, as it had no relation to her current, anxious mind. "But anyway. This Saturday, I invited the entire Coleman family over for a little bonfire and barbe-cue. I hope you don't mind?"

Reese rubbed his temples. "All right. Tell me what you need me to buy at the store."

"You're wonderful," Oriana said, fetching a notepad to make a list. "What would I do without you?"

On Saturday morning at eleven, the first of the party guests arrived. Nora appeared through the trees lining Oriana and Alan's homes, her arms laden with beer, wine, and potato salad, and her smile serene.

"Nora! You're early!" Oriana was in the backyard, setting up tables and chairs. The Coleman guests weren't officially set to arrive until one.

"I figured you'd need some help," Nora said. "Alan will be over soon, too. Alan?" She called through the trees until Alan popped out, his forehead slightly burnt from his hours of gardening the very last assortment of zucchini, radishes, and corn before they closed the garden for the season. "Oriana needs you!"

Oriana laughed and glanced around the backyard. It seemed there was always something else to do, more yard tasks, more things to clean. Ultimately, she asked Alan to chop firewood for the afternoon and evening ahead, which he gladly did, even removing his shirt so that his back glistened as he swung the ax over and over again, splintering the wood. As Nora stirred up iced tea on the back porch, she watched him unabashedly and told Oriana, "I never thought I'd fall in love again. And now, look at this man I'm dating! He's like Paul Newman!"

Oriana had never once compared Alan to Paul Newman, not in all the years she'd lived beside him. But beauty was in the eye of the beholder, she knew. And it warmed her heart to watch Nora fall deeper in love, especially this late in life.

"How did it go with meeting Roland and Grant?" Nora asked finally, escaping her reverie.

"It was lovely," Oriana admitted. "I was really nervous. But they opened their arms to us, stuffed us with delicious food, and let us stay the night, even. When we woke up, Roland's wife, Estelle, fed us again with pancakes, bacon, and eggs. I was surprised Derek's boat didn't sink when he brought us back home."

Nora cackled. She, too, had a complicated history with the Colemans. Her only son, Marcus, had been best friends with Charlie as teenagers, but had died in a car accident at seventeen. Charlie had been driving.

That single moment changed Nora's life forever. Still, that summer had brought healing for all of them, especially after Nora's great-nephew, Jax, had wrecked a car Charlie's daughter had been in. Forgiveness had become paramount. Nora and Charlie had finally begun to speak again.

Because they'd taken a ferry all together, the Nantucket Colemans arrived all at once: Roland and Estelle, Sam, her boyfriend, Derek, and her daughters, Rachelle and Darcy; Hilary, her boyfriend, Marc, and her daughter, Aria; Charlie, his wife, Shawna, and their two daughters and son; plus Grant, Katrina, their daughter, Sophie, and her boyfriend Patrick; along with their other daughter, Ida, and her husband Rick, whose daughters were away at college.

As they streamed through the backyard, Alexa, Benny, and Reese came out the backdoor, all dressed in flannel and autumn jackets, wearing vibrant smiles. Reese clapped the backs of Grant and Roland happily and asked if they wanted a beer to go with this autumn breeze. They agreed and soon gathered around the flickering bonfire, chatting about baseball.

"Hilary! I'm so glad to see you!" Oriana hugged Hilary, who wore sunglasses over her eyes to protect them after her recent surgery.

"And you!" Hilary laughed. "Everything's still a little

blurry for me, but I should be in the all-clear by November or so."

"And Aria? How's the interior design work coming along?" Oriana asked.

"We just wrapped a job out in San Francisco," Aria explained, linking her fingers with her mother's.

"Aria finished it, actually," Hilary bragged. "You should have seen her save me a few times the past couple of months, as my eyes were failing me."

"I don't know how we got so lucky with our daughters," Oriana said, watching as Alexa lifted Benny against her chest and twirled in the grass.

"Oh, Meghan's here!" Sam called, bouncing toward the backyard gate to hug Oriana's sister, who led their father, Chuck, her husband, Hugo, their children, Eva and Theo, and Eva's boyfriend, Finn.

With a terrible jolt in her stomach, Oriana realized that she hadn't seen Meghan in perhaps seven days, maybe eight. She knew this was her fault. She'd fought to make herself feel busy, to fill her head with work, and on the way, she'd lost track of Meghan. There had been ignored text messages and missed calls. And now, as Meghan approached her, her smile waned, as though she was afraid to see Oriana. This broke her heart.

"Hi, Meghan." Oriana cupped her sister's elbow.

Under her breath, Meghan whispered, "Are you doing okay, sis?"

Oriana's smile faltered. "I'm really good. I'm so glad everyone could come out to the party."

Meghan nodded stiffly and gave Oriana a strange look. Oriana knew better than to try to escape Meghan's watchful eye. Looking back, it was bizarre that she'd ever been able to get away with the original crime, as Meghan had been directly beside her, watching the events surrounding it play out. Perhaps Meghan knew what Oriana had done. Perhaps Meghan was the blackmailer?

No, that was impossible.

"I just haven't seen much of you lately," Meghan continued, unwilling to let Oriana off the hook. "I've been worried."

Oriana set her jaw. Under Meghan's watchful eye, she hardly knew how to act, as Meghan would call her out immediately for lying.

But a moment later, Roland approached with a beer to say hello. His nervous smile proved that he still wasn't fully comfortable around them yet, but he wanted to work on it.

"How was New York?" he asked Oriana.

"Oh, it was fine," Oriana said, waving her hand.

"She's being modest," Reese interjected. "She just learned she's the recipient of a huge award."

Roland's eyes widened. "You're kidding. Congratulations, Oriana!"

Meghan shifted her weight, giving Oriana a hurt look. *Why hadn't Oriana mentioned the award to Meghan?*

"We should make a toast," Meghan said, her voice wavering, as though she was on the verge of tears. And Oriana understood why. After all, through thick and thin, Meghan and Oriana had told one another nearly everything. Oriana suddenly blocking Meghan out probably felt horrific.

But if Oriana told Meghan what was really going on, what would Meghan say? Oriana was terrified of the look in Meghan's eye, of the realization that Oriana was little more than a fraud.

Meghan filled a glass with wine and raised it toward

the sparkling September sky. "Everyone! I've just learned about my sister's remarkable accolade. Very soon, the city of New York will recognize her for the astonishing art dealer she is and always has been. The fact that she's been able to do her work while here, in Martha's Vineyard, where she's been such a dear friend and sister to me all these years, is truly spectacular."

Oriana felt the words like a knife. She knew that Meghan was trying to make a point, to remind Oriana that she wouldn't be abandoned.

Both branches of the Coleman family raised their glasses of iced tea, soda, cans of beer, and red cups filled with white wine to toast Oriana, who blushed and bowed her head.

"Thank you for helping me celebrate, everyone," Oriana said. "I don't know how I could have done any of this without my sweet and very understanding family." Oriana shot Meghan a look that meant, *I'm doing the best I can, and I love you.*

It was strange that sisters could communicate with one another without saying anything at all.

Eventually, Oriana found herself around the bonfire, seated on a lawn chair, chatting with Estelle, Sam, Hilary, and Shawna, all of whom were incredibly sweet women and remarkable additions to Oriana's family. The men played corn hole across the yard, hollering out with excitement or regret, depending on how the beanbag had landed.

"Roland hasn't been able to shut up about our dinner with you," Estelle said to Oriana, lowering her voice slightly.

"I've thought about it a lot, too," Oriana offered.

"He can't get over how 'brilliant' his little sisters are,"

Estelle said with a laugh. "I think he's bragged about you to almost everyone we've seen since then."

Oriana's cheeks burned. Great. Roland was but another person she would disappoint when the truth came out. She never thought she'd regret forging a relationship with her half-brothers.

Suddenly, Oriana's phone buzzed in her pocket. When she pulled it out, the screen read: RITA.

"I have to take this," Oriana said, fleeing the backyard and entering the house. "Rita?"

Oh gosh. She needed answers. She needed them now.

"Hi, Oriana." Rita's voice was bright and chipper. "Do you have time to talk?"

Oriana was at the staircase, darting up the steps to get as far away from her family as possible. "I do." She tried not to sound breathless, even though she was.

"Great. I've found the person you've been looking for."

At the top of the staircase, Oriana nearly fell back in surprise. "You're kidding."

"I'm not."

"How?"

"It was a complicated procedure, I have to say," Rita explained. "I normally operate with people in the United States, so the fact that she'd initially fled to Argentina made things much more difficult. It seems like she spent about eighteen months in Argentina, then some time in France, a few months in Egypt, then a couple of years on an island off the coast of Croatia before she wound up in Thailand."

Oriana's eyes widened in surprise. "Thailand?" It seemed like another planet.

"An island called Ko Tao. I can send you the address of her place after this phone call."

Oriana's head spun. "And she's okay?"

"I didn't actually make it to Thailand to speak with her," Rita said. "And she doesn't know I found her, either. You should see some of the elaborate methods she used to try to stay hidden."

"You must be a very good private detective." Oriana wasn't sure what else to say.

"I've been around a long time," Rita said. "Unlucky for Brea, she used a lot of techniques that a recent guy I found also used, so I'd been through this before."

Oriana sputtered. "Can you tell me anything about her? Anything at all?"

"Not much else," Rita admitted. "But she's there. And it doesn't look like she's headed anywhere else any time soon."

"So, I guess I'd better buy a plane ticket," Oriana breathed.

"Pack your swimsuit," Rita joked. "I know this isn't a pleasurable trip— but it's gorgeous there. You had better enjoy it."

Chapter Thirteen

October 1998

It had been two weeks since Kenny's diagnosis, and everything had gone from bad to worse. Frequently at work, Brea hid in the bathroom to sob and scream into wads of toilet paper, then redo her makeup to perfection, trying as hard as she could to look the part of a successful art dealer on the brink of the rest of her life. In reality, her life was a nightmare.

"You ready to go out again tonight?" Oriana walked past Brea's desk, smiling. "Nick says he put us on the guest list at Marco's." She paused, then bent down to add, "I think Nick's going to close that deal on the Hedgehog drawing. Half a million dollars! Not bad. Plus, I think Nick is really fun, don't you?"

Brea congratulated Oriana on the near-sale and agreed to go out, despite the fact that she wasn't sure she trusted Nick. He and Oriana had gotten very chummy very quickly, in a way that suggested to Brea that Nick wanted something out of Oriana. Maybe he wanted better deals on art. Maybe he wanted her "in" with some high rollers like Walter. Or maybe he just had a crush on her, which probably wasn't terrible in and of itself. Oriana was head-over-heels with Reese and would never consider cheating.

"I bought a new dress for you," Oriana said just before she left Brea's desk. "It's a sexy thing, so make sure Kenny sees you in it before you go out." She winked.

Oriana was on top of the world. Walter had agreed to the four-million-dollar deal, and she was in talks to sell several other pieces of art— sculptures and wall murals that had been cut off actual buildings, puppets, and diaries from important, now-dead artists. Since the diagnosis, Brea had done her best to keep up with her, to attend every important lunch and dinner, to fetch Oriana's snacks when she had low blood sugar, and to crack jokes with the clients when Oriana had to go into the next room to take a call from another client. Over and over again, Oriana had told Brea, "It's going to be worth it soon when we're both working together on Martha's Vineyard."

But the concept of this "happy life" in Martha's Vineyard was beginning to look less and less likely, at least for Brea and Kenny. The doctor had said he would die if he didn't get his kidney transplant soon. Even though dialysis would buy him some time, it was still running short. He was on a list, but the list was very long, filled with names of other people whose lives were similarly hopeless, and once his name did come up, they wouldn't have the money to accept the surgery.

Brea had considered asking Oriana for more money. But Oriana didn't have the money for something like kidney surgery, not this early in her career. Because they were a "real family," Oriana and Reese had health insurance. They'd set up their lives in ways Brea and Kenny hadn't even considered, because they'd thought they were young and healthy— nothing could touch them.

Although they'd sworn her to secrecy, Kenny's mother had learned of Kenny's illness and soon appeared on Brea and Kenny's doorstep to help out. This had resulted in hours and hours of Valerie scream-crying in the bathroom, which had only added to the doom and gloom of the apartment. Eventually, though, she'd figured out how she was needed and where, which had given Brea a little bit of breathing room.

Kenny told her endlessly she needed to keep her job. And it devastated her to realize that he said these things, mostly because he assumed she would live long after him — and she needed something to live for.

On the night Brea agreed to go out to Marco's club with Nick and Oriana, she dressed in the bathroom, did her makeup, and stepped into the living room to see Valerie and Kenny on the couch. Kenny was skeletal and so sick, and Valerie was crocheting a blanket angrily, her eyes on the news. Valerie had made it clear she didn't approve of Brea's career, as it took her "out to clubs" too often. Brea hated that aspect of it, too, but she didn't like Valerie enough to agree with her verbally.

Ultimately, Brea felt lost— more lost than she'd ever been. And she didn't have anyone to turn to.

"Have a wonderful night, baby," Kenny said as Brea leaned down to kiss him. "See you later."

Regret and guilt were heavy on Brea's shoulders as she walked out into the night to meet Oriana and Nick. But when she reached the nightclub to stand in line behind Oriana and Nick, the bouncer surprised them with news.

"You two are on the list. She's not." He pointed at Brea.

Oriana's jaw dropped. "Nick? Did you forget to put Brea on the list?"

Nick frowned. "There must be some mistake."

But the bouncer wouldn't hear of it. "The list is the list. You two get in or get out."

Oriana reached toward Brea and squeezed her hand. "I'll come with you wherever you want to go."

But Brea heard the hesitance in Oriana's voice. She knew that Oriana wanted to see and be seen in such a place, to rub shoulders with future clients, and to ultimately woo Nick into handing over half a million.

Besides. The thought of having one night off from all of that pleased Brea to no end.

"You go in," Brea urged her. "Kenny has the night off tonight, so I'll just go back home and hang out."

"Are you sure?"

"Definitely," Brea said. "Have fun."

Brea turned on her heel and rushed back out into the night, listening as Nick cried out, "Let's go, Oriana," and tugged her inside. Again, Brea had a strange suspicion about that guy and felt nearly one hundred percent certain that he hadn't put her name on the list on purpose. Right now, she didn't care. In fact, so far from Kenny and Valerie, miles and miles from Martha's Vineyard, and drifting away from Oriana, she wasn't sure what she felt like. Certainly, she didn't feel like herself.

Goodness, wasn't it nice not to feel like herself for once?

Brea walked for over a mile until her feet screamed in

her shoes, and she entered a bar that sold beer from the tap and not-so-fancy wine. Somebody played Steely Dan on the jukebox, and people hung on the bar top, singing the lyrics and laughing with one another. It had little to do with Oriana's "swanky" New York. It seemed more related to home.

Brea sat on a bar stool and ordered herself a beer, which she hadn't drunk in ages. The bartender placed it on the counter and then left her alone. Brea sipped with her eyes closed, trying to shove away her fears, her sorrows. She was just a woman in her twenties. She was just an anonymous woman in New York City.

"You must really like that beer."

Brea's eyes snapped open at the sound of a man's voice. Three stools down sat a guy in his late thirties, maybe, with scruffy brown hair and big puppy dog eyes. He smiled at her and raised his beer, adding, "I didn't mean to interrupt."

Brea was silent for a moment. The guy's attention was warm and nourishing, a reminder that nobody had looked at her like that, outside of the context of her life, in a long time. It wasn't that she was attracted to him— her love for Kenny was too strong. But it was lovely to be seen.

"You're right. I do like this beer," Brea said. "I feel like I've been drinking cosmopolitans for weeks, non-stop. I've had enough."

The man laughed. "You're a Cosmo girl?"

"Not really," Brea said. "I work in an industry that demands you dress a certain way, drink a certain drink, and schmooze."

The man winced. "That's just about every industry in New York, don't you think?"

"I don't know. I haven't lived here very long."

The man nodded toward the stool beside her, questioning if he could get closer. She nodded, and he stood, walked around, and sat down. So close up, he was less handsome than he'd been down the bar, and his teeth were slightly yellowed, probably from smoking. Everyone in New York City smoked.

"And where did you come from?" the guy asked.

"Martha's Vineyard," she answered.

"That's heaven on earth, isn't it?"

Brea nodded. She genuinely believed it was, which begged the question: *why had she ever left?* Maybe, if she and Kenny had never come here, he never would have gotten sick. Maybe it was all her fault.

"I'm Neal," he said, sticking out his hand for her to shake. Brea did, introducing herself as well.

"You look like you're dressed up for a place a lot fancier than this," Neal said.

Brea blushed. "I had plans to go out, but they fell through."

"Did a guy bail on you?"

"No. I was going out for a client, but he forgot to put me on the guest list."

Neal cocked his head. "Really? That's strange. I guess that means you lost that deal?"

"I'm an assistant," Brea explained. "I'm working for my best friend. An art dealer. She's moving up the ranks quickly and hoping to take me with her."

"I see." Neal sipped his beer. "And your best friend is from Martha's Vineyard, too?"

"Yes," Brea said.

"Why is she so much more advanced in her career?"

"She moved out here before me," Brea explained, then paused for a moment before adding, "And I was trying to make it as an artist for a while, which sounds so embarrassing. I mean, who would ever want to buy my art?"

"Are you kidding? Some of the stuff these art dealers sell is atrocious," Neal said.

Brea's smile widened. "Right? Almost every new piece that Oriana shows me makes me shake my head. I can't believe anyone would ever buy it, let alone make it in the first place. And then, she tells me the price, and it's in the one, two, three-million-dollar range!"

Neal's eyes flickered. "Okay, that is ridiculous! People place very strange prices on material items. It's obnoxious."

"I keep thinking that."

"So, your best friend's name is Oriana?"

Brea nodded. "Oriana Coleman. She decided to go with her maiden name, professionally."

"I think I've heard of the Colemans before. There are Colemans on Nantucket, right?" Neal said.

"The Colemans that live on Nantucket are different. Well, sort of."

"Sort of?"

"It's a long story," Brea said, stirring in embarrassment. Chuck, Oriana's father, had nothing to do with Brea— and she didn't want to gossip. Still, it did fascinate her that Chuck had had this whole other life in Nantucket, which he'd abandoned for Oriana's mother, Mia. It made her head spin, thinking people could be so cruel to those they loved.

"So, the plan is that you'll have your own clients after you're her assistant for a while?" Neal asked, rebounding the conversation.

"That's the plan right now," Brea said. "We want to

move back to Martha's Vineyard to work together, outside of the business here in New York, which means no more guest lists. No more clubs."

"You seem pretty happy about that," Neal said with a laugh.

"More than you know."

Neal dropped his head back. "You've probably seen some incredible things in this industry. You'll only get better at the business side of things as you go along." He raised his drink to salute her. "I'm pulling for you, Brea. It seems to me that you're damn good at your job, if only because you don't have all this New York City pretentiousness. That will take you far."

Brea glowed at his compliments, allowing herself to fall away from the devastation of her life and into this imaginary one that she and Neal created at this bar. It had been a long time since she'd felt more important than Oriana. But right now, she would milk it for all it was worth.

Chapter Fourteen

Present Day

Reaching Ko Tao, Brea's island in Thailand, was much more complicated than Oriana had initially planned. Excited, her thoughts going in a million different directions, she booked a flight from Boston to Bangkok, explaining to Reese that she needed to meet a client in that exotic city so far from home. But immediately after she'd booked the flights, she realized Bangkok was quite far from Ko Tao and that she'd need to take an additional flight, plus a boat, to reach the island. With the end of September just around the corner, her stomach performed somersaults. She didn't have much time before the blackmailer revealed everything.

Because he was a wonderful, kind, and loyal husband, Reese dropped Oriana off at the airport the following morning, kissed her goodbye, and told her to eat plenty of mango for him. Oriana swayed in his arms, woozy, as she'd been too nervous to eat.

"This is why you're getting that award," Reese said.

"You go above and beyond for art. It's incredible to watch."

The first flight took Oriana from Boston to Istanbul— a horrific and very long period during which she was unable to sleep or concentrate on a film for longer than a few minutes. Although she'd purchased first class, flying was still not as comfortable as her bed at home— and she dreaded what awaited her in Ko Tao.

One thought had begun to rise to the surface: that maybe Brea was the blackmailer, and she'd sent those letters to force Oriana to fund her life in Thailand. Brea had disappeared herself many, many years ago. She probably needed money at this point.

If that was true, was it possible Brea knew Oriana was coming to see her? Maybe Rita had walked directly into Brea's trap.

Then again, Brea had never been a villainous mastermind. She'd always been an artistic, soft, and very kind soul. She'd had to leave the United States; there had been no other option for her. But Oriana had always imagined that after that, she'd found somewhere beautiful to live, perhaps fallen in love with someone, and had a few babies. Rita hadn't had any information about that. Maybe it was partially true?

Then again, if Brea had had children, that meant she probably needed money all the more.

In Istanbul, Oriana sat at an airport bar, nursing a glass of wine, and texting the people she loved, so far away on Martha's Vineyard. Even Roland chimed in, wishing her good luck on her big trip.

Meghan had written:

> Hey! Just wanted to say congrats on the big sale in Bangkok. Question (and don't take this the wrong way): is there something wrong? Ever since we returned from New York, I've felt like you're avoiding me for some reason. I know, I know. It's not all about me. But I'm slightly worried that you're angry, and I would love to know what I did wrong so I can fix it.

Oriana closed her eyes and pressed her phone against her chest. She had to make it seem that everything was fine.

> ORIANA: Don't worry about a thing! I've been stressed with work stuff (no excuse, I know). Let's catch up when I'm back, okay?

> ORIANA: I'll bring you a great souvenir.

On the flight from Istanbul to Bangkok, Oriana was just tired enough to slip in and out of consciousness for hours, frequently falling into nightmares before bursting awake. In the dreams, peers of hers in the city were shaming her, telling her they'd always known she was a fraud, that they'd always suspected she'd gotten where she was criminally.

"Are you all right, madame?" A French stewardess paused and looked down at her in her airline seat.

"What? Oh. Yes. I'm fine. I'm..." Oriana sputtered. "Could you please pour me some wine?"

The stewardess returned with a glass, and Oriana sipped it, trying to steady her anxious mind. It was impossible to know what time it was or where she was in the world. Outside, it was dark. She would land close to midnight. The entire trip was twenty-two hours long and far from over.

At customs, Oriana placed her American passport on the counter and watched as the customs employee scanned it, glanced at her, and stamped a page toward the back. She was in. *Had Brea come in just like this? How had she hidden herself so well? Even Rita had been impressed with her tactics.*

Oriana couldn't fathom how anyone could hide away this deep into the twenty-first century. Her phone tracked everywhere she went. She frequently posted photographs to social media. Not only did she feel she had nothing to hide (except for the 1998 incident), she felt eager to share her life.

After her suitcase arrived at baggage claim, Oriana wheeled it out into a balmy night. Taxis lined up like shiny yellow beetles, and one of the drivers hurried forward to take her suitcase. Her hotel was thirty minutes from the airport, a blissful drive during which she gazed out at the impossible darkness and listened to the Thai radio station.

Oriana's hotel was quaint and very comfortable. The hotel concierge was careful to tell her they'd ordered "western mattresses" for each room, as traditional Thai mattresses were hard as cement. Apparently, previous customers had complained.

That night, Oriana slept like a rock and awoke at eight, her heart thudding with expectation. That after-noon, she had another flight to Ko Samui, followed by an immediate boat to Ko Tao.

Because she was twelve hours ahead of Martha's Vineyard, it was eight p.m. yesterday there. That meant Reese was still up.

His voice was welcoming and bright when he answered her call. "There she is! Our world traveler. How were the flights?"

"Exhausting," Oriana said, smiling into the phone. "I couldn't sleep very much on the plane."

"I'm sorry to hear that. I hope you don't have too many meetings today?"

"Not many," Oriana said.

"How's Bangkok?"

Oriana's hotel wasn't fully in Bangkok, as she needed to get back to the airport. Out her window was rolling hills and a line of shimmering blue— the ocean.

"It's crazy here," Oriana lied, remembering what she'd learned of Bangkok. "It feels like the city never calms down."

"I bet."

"What are you up to? How's home?"

Reese eased her mind with his boring roundup of what he and Benny had done, what they'd eaten, and the television shows he was watching. Oriana was grateful for the comfort of schedules, family, and going through the boring details of everyday life with her soul mate. She would have given almost anything to be there with them.

The flight to the island of Ko Samui was brief and easy. Out the window, Oriana watched the plane glide toward a lush green island in the midst of a turquoise sea. It looked like a Windows screensaver rather than real life.

She was beginning to understand why Brea had picked Thailand to hide out.

The boat to Ko Samui was a squat little ferry with very little speed. As they went, Oriana overheard an English tourist telling a friend that in another boat, they'd dropped all the tourists off still in the water, and he'd had to carry his bag over his head. "The water was up to my chest!" Oriana imagined the boat employees asking her to do that, to just "get out" when the boat hadn't reached the shore. She would probably laugh at such a ridiculous request. After all, her clothes were Dior, and her shoes were Louboutin. No, she didn't fit in with the rest of these tourists in their elephant pants and tank tops. But maybe she'd forgotten how to look casual after so many years of having to dress the part of a very important art dealer.

In fact, she couldn't remember the last time she'd gone somewhere without makeup, or a little under-dressed, or without putting on a pair of expensive earrings. It had just become her state of permanent being.

Luckily, this particular boat pulled up to a dock, then secured its lines and dropped a ramp to allow its guests to walk onto dry land. It was just past five in the afternoon, and the sun was especially orange and hot across Oriana's shoulders. Her large Chanel sunglasses protected her eyes, but she felt her forehead begin to crisp, despite her sunscreen.

It wasn't as simple to get a taxi here on Ko Tao as it had been at the airport. It seemed most people's form of transportation was a motorbike, and Oriana was too frightened to drive one herself. Besides, she couldn't exactly strap her suitcase to the back of one, could she?

Turns out, it was possible. A man with a motorcycle flagged her down, read Brea's address on her cell phone, nodded, strapped her suitcase to the back of his motorcycle, and then explained the pay was 100 BAT, which was the equivalent of three dollars. Oriana said it was a deal.

Oriana hadn't been on a motorcycle since she'd been a teenager. Reese had borrowed one from a friend and taken her all over the island. Most of that time, she'd filled

Reese's ears with her screams, and he'd refused to take her again. She hadn't minded.

So many years later— approximately thirty-three, Oriana had more nerve and confidence. She held loosely to the Thai man's torso and felt herself be tugged forward, down both paved streets and dirt streets, past waving palm trees, alongside white sandy beaches. For a little while, she allowed herself to pretend she was on a solo vacation, during which she would do some real, solid "thinking." She'd never had time to go on a vacation by herself before. She'd always wondered if people who did that got lonely.

About twenty minutes after he'd picked her up, the Thai man stalled at the edge of a very sandy path.

"Can't go more," the man explained to her.

"Oh. Um?" Oriana spun with confusion as the Thai man pointed down the path and said, "There."

Behind the swaying palm trees, toward the shimmering ocean, was a stretch of shacks. None of them were especially beautiful, but they were taken care of, their rooftops thatched, their porches clean. Oriana slid off the motorcycle as the driver removed her suitcase and placed it beside her. With a jump, she remembered to pay him and passed him two hundred BAT rather than one hundred. He was pleased but confused.

The suitcase was quite difficult to wheel through the sand. Oriana did her best to tug it as sweat dripped down her neck, through her armpits, and down her back. When she reached the edge of the dirt path, she paused to gasp for air. The sun seemed to taunt her, refusing to grow colder or reach the horizon. *How did people live like this?* The humidity made the air milkshake thick.

And as she cursed the air, the heat, her useless limbs,

and her inability to go forward, a figure burst from one of the porches and stood on the steps, staring down at her. The figure had long salt and pepper hair, a muscular frame, a face without makeup, and open, honest eyes.

Oriana would have recognized Brea anywhere.

But she hadn't imagined seeing her again would feel like a knife through her stomach.

For a moment, Oriana and Brea stared at one another, shocked. It was clear Brea hadn't expected Oriana to come, that Brea hadn't caught onto Rita's tracking. Oriana expected Brea to say something, to demand what she was doing there, or— worse— to tell her to get off her property.

But instead, Brea jumped down the steps and ran toward Oriana, closing the distance between them. And before Oriana could think of anything to say or any excuse, Brea threw her arms around Oriana, pulled her close, and wept into her shoulder.

Chapter Fifteen

October 1998

With Oriana off with Nick at yet another exclusive nightclub, and Valerie and Kenny back at home, Brea found herself at that same bar with Neal. It had been a week since they'd met one another, a gruesome week of Kenny's illness, doctors' appointments, glitzy meetings with Oriana's clients, and art, so much art that, to Brea, looked heinous and not worthy of anyone's time.

"You should see this four-million-dollar piece," Brea said, shaking her head over a glass of beer. "I mean, Neal, it's insane to me. It's a few slashes of green, violet, and blue, and when this billionaire guy looks at it, he wells up with tears."

Neal cackled, dropping his head back. "What billionaire guy?"

"I'm sure you've heard of him. It seems like everybody has heard of him except for me."

"Maybe I have. What's his name?"

"Walter Billington."

Neal almost spat out his beer with laughter. "*The* Walter Billington? You're kidding. You know him?"

"I don't know him. I've been out with him a few times. He's nice, sort of. For a rich guy." Brea shrugged, recognizing that Neal's eyes glowed just a little bit more than they had, that he now regarded her with more respect, if only because she'd been in the shadow of the great Walter Billington a few times.

"Nice for a rich guy." Neal laughed again.

"Yeah. He's cool to talk to," Brea added. "He doesn't ignore me like all the other rich guys we meet. Most of them just talk to Oriana, and I'm supposed to sit there and pretend I don't exist."

"That sounds terrible," Neal said quietly.

Brea shrugged.

"So, now that Walter's bought this four-million-dollar painting, do you think he'll buy more stuff from you guys?"

"The purchase hasn't gone through yet," Brea explained, feeling confident about how much she now understood the business. "The process is so much longer than you'd think. There are piles of paperwork, most of which I have to fill out myself."

"Oooh. Nobody likes paperwork."

Neal waved down the bartender to order another round of beers. Brea was slightly woozy on the stool, weaving back and forth. Perhaps she'd already drunk too much. Perhaps she should have eaten dinner.

"Man, I'd love to see this green, violet, and blue mess of a painting," Neal said, his eyes flashing. "If it's enough for Walter Billington, then it has to be great."

"You calling me a liar?" Brea joked.

Neal cackled. "I would never. I have a hunch your taste is a lot like mine. But hey? Expensive is expensive, and men like Walter like to throw their weight around." Neal sipped his new beer, eyeing her. "Where do you keep that painting?"

Brea waved her hand. "It's behind four padlocks."

"Wow. Impressive."

"Nobody's getting in there to steal that horrible assault to your eyes," Brea said.

Neal smiled, and Brea felt as though she floated from the stool and into the air above the bar. Never in her life had she flirted with anyone who wasn't Kenny. *But was this flirting? Was she smiling too much?* Oh, she couldn't wrong Kenny like this. Her smile faltered, and she drank too much of her beer, her thoughts swirling.

"Hey! Easy, tiger." Neal touched her shoulder kindly. "There's plenty more beer where that came from. You don't have to drink it all at once."

Brea shivered as she set back down the beer. "Sorry."

"You don't have to be sorry." Neal frowned. "Man, I can't help but think that someone in your life is treating you badly. Making you feel like you're not enough."

Brea eyed him nervously. "I guess there's a lot about my life you don't understand."

"I know we don't know each other that well," Neal said. "And I don't mean to be creepy. But you can talk to me, you know?" He coughed, then added, "Don't worry. I see the engagement ring on your finger. I know you would never go behind your man's back. And heck, I wouldn't want you to!"

Brea blinked back tears and breathed a sigh of relief. "He works nights. He's a chef."

"Wow. A chef. I love a man who knows how to cook,"

Neal said. "Maybe we can all get together some time? I can bring my on-again, off-again girlfriend, Janine. She loves to cook, too."

"Where is she tonight?"

"She works nights as a nurse," Neal said, his smile fading slightly.

"What a generous person," Brea offered.

"Yes. She's got a heart of gold, my girl." Neal took a long drink of beer.

For the rest of the night, Brea and Neal talked about the important people in their lives— about Neal's girlfriend, about Kenny. Brea spoke of Kenny the way she might have pre-diagnosis, about how full of life he was. And Neal told of Janine, a vivacious woman who wanted to save the world.

As they paid up that night, Neal asked, "What do you say we go for a walk in a few days? We don't always have to drink. Besides, I get the sense that we're pretty lonely when our loves are hard at work."

"I'd like that," Brea said, grateful for a friend.

A few days later, when Oriana was with her children and Reese, Brea met Neal in Greenwich Village for a long walk. It was a gorgeous October blue-skied day, and leaves twitched from trees and streamed to the ground, coating the sidewalk with mush. Before she'd left, Brea had kissed Kenny with her eyes closed, and he'd fallen asleep on the couch while Valerie had whispered dangerously toward Brea, asking, "How on earth are we going to keep my baby alive?" Brea hadn't known what to say.

All she wanted in the world was for Valerie to leave. For things to go back to normal. But "normal" was a distant land.

As she and Neal walked and talked on this October

afternoon, he told her stories of Janine again. Brea spoke at length about work, about the paperwork she had to fill out, and again, about Walter Billington, who was in Tokyo for the next two weeks, but would come back to fetch his painting and have it hung in his apartment on the Upper East Side.

"How exciting," Neal said.

"Isn't it?" Brea rolled her eyes.

Neal stopped at the corner and squeezed his hands into fists. "Brea, I'm dying to ask you something."

Brea's heart thumped. "What's that?"

"I'm just so curious about this painting. I assume there are no photographs taken of it?"

"There are some photographs back at the office," Brea said. "Want to walk that way? I can run up to grab them."

"Okay. But I don't want to go in there," Neal said. "I'm not a fan of those artsy folks."

Brea laughed. "I know. They have a terrible air about them, don't they? I'll just bring them down, and we can hit up that bar near the office so you can get a full look. But we have to be careful! Nobody else at the bar can see them."

"Of course," Neal said. "We'll be discrete."

At the office, Brea hurried upstairs, found the folder of photographs in Oriana's drawer, then returned to the street, panting. Nobody had said a word to her in the office. After all, she was just an assistant. She hardly existed.

"Brilliant! You're brilliant. I'm buying you a drink," Neal said.

They entered a dive bar, where they could sit in the corner to pore over the photographs. Brea placed the folder of photographs on the table and did a small drum-roll over them to up the drama.

"Put the beers on another table," she ordered Neal. "If we spill beer on these photographs, Oriana will have my head."

"She'll never see these photographs again," Neal pointed out. "The painting is sold! The deal is done!"

Brea grimaced. He was mostly right. "Still. She won't be happy if she notices that I took them out of the office."

"Whatever." Neal placed both beers on a separate table, then opened the folder, his eyes widening. In the first photograph, there was the painting in all its tragedy—greens, violets, and blues in wild dashes to illustrate something that could have been a face but probably was not. "My god, Brea. You weren't kidding."

Brea leaned forward, trying to see the painting as though for the first time. "Right? It's sort of..."

"Atrocious?" Neal tried. "The dashes of a madman?"

Brea chortled. "I know." Under her breath, she added, "Can you believe someone is willing to pay four million for it?"

"It's insanity," Neal said. He then leaned back in his chair, cackling, leafing through the photographs. "Why are there so many? There's one taken of every angle!"

But as Neal laughed and carried on, he leaned a little too far back in his chair, then fell completely into the table with the beers on it, thus knocking both beers to the ground. Immediately, Brea sprung up, panicked, eyeing the bartender. "Shoot! Shoot!" Neal was on the ground, and Brea was beside him, helping him up as the bartender approached.

"Are you okay over here?" The bartender hurried with a rag and then sighed at the mess. "I'll grab a mop."

"I can help you," Brea heard herself say, ever the people pleaser. Quickly, she tugged Neal back to his feet as Neal mumbled words of apology.

"I'm such an idiot! I don't know what came over me," he said, smiling a sloppy, handsome smile.

"Don't worry about it," Brea said. "It can happen."

"I guess I was just so overwhelmed with this silly painting," he said as he stood up, adjusting himself over the table.

"I understand." Brea chuckled and hurried to collect the mop. By the time she got back to the table, Neal had cleaned himself up, placed the photographs back in the folder, and begun to apologize profusely to the bartender.

"It's a rare thing that my customers make a mess and offer to clean it up for me," the bartender said with a shrug. "As far as I'm concerned, you both have earned free drinks from this." He then set about pouring them another round.

"Let me do that," Neal said, extending a hand to take the mop.

Brea couldn't remember the last time someone had offered to do something for her, to go out of their way to make her life easier. Her cheeks hot, she passed the mop over and watched as he swept it over the beer, whistling. When he finished, the bartender returned with their "free" round, and everyone was smiling.

"To my favorite customers," the bartender said.

"Man," Neal said as he sat back down. "You really weren't lying about that painting."

Brea sighed. "I wish I had been."

"It just makes me so curious about your art," Neal said. "The stuff you were making before you got into this silly industry. I mean, if that's worth four million dollars, what you created should be worth eight million! Or more!"

Brea laughed. "Don't flatter me. You haven't even seen my stuff."

"But I would like to," Neal said, leaning back in his chair. "I have this strange feeling that, well..." He trailed off.

"What is it?" Again, Brea was frightened that he wanted to confess his feelings, that he'd realized he couldn't be "just friends" with her. That was something she couldn't accommodate.

"I just keep feeling like we're going to be friends for a long time. The thing is, back when I was a teenager, my best friend in the world was my sister, Jocelyn. We did everything together. Nintendo, bike rides, pancake eating contests. Everything." Neal's eyes clouded. "But she died right after we both got into college. It was devastating for me. I had to drop out. I had to reconfigure how I felt about the world."

Brea's heart shattered. Neal understood the density of loss— the way it weighted you down. She hadn't yet lost Kenny— but a part of her had begun to prepare for it, as it was impossible they'd be able to afford his surgery.

"Anyway, being with you reminds me of who I was back then," Neal went on. "Carefree."

Brea wanted to tell him that being with him was a similar experience for her, that it reminded her of the person she'd been before Kenny's diagnosis. But she just didn't feel up to talking about it. So, she said, "Thank you for telling me about Jocelyn. It sounds so painful."

"It was," Neal affirmed. "And it was so, so long ago now. I don't know that I'll ever get over it."

Brea understood. She knew that, once Kenny was gone, she would never recover. Not completely.

Over the next week, Brea hung with Neal a handful of times— for coffee, some hot dogs on the street, or to enjoy a couple of beers at the end of a long day. As Oriana grew increasingly frantic and stressed in their work environment, Brea had begun to think of Neal as her last link to normalcy. He made her laugh. He surprised her with her favorite chocolate bars, asked her questions about her family, and never, ever made her feel less-than or unintelligent.

But everything fell apart just like that.

Neal invited Brea to his apartment for the first time, explaining that his girlfriend wanted to meet her. "She's heard so much about you and wants to make sure you're real and not a figment of my imagination. Plus, I think you two would get along well."

Brea considered this to be proof that *When Harry Met Sally* was incorrect. Men and women could befriend one another without complications. She and Neal were proof of that.

But when Brea arrived at Neal's apartment, his girlfriend was not there after all.

"She got called into the hospital last minute," Neal explained regretfully.

The apartment was about three times as big as the one Brea shared with Kenny and his mother, with two bathrooms and a view of Central Park. It seemed incredible to her that such a rich and successful man drank at dive bars with her and shelled out quarters for jukebox songs.

"You want a drink?" Neal asked as she hung up her coat.

"Um. Sure?"

"I was thinking about making Negronis," he explained.

Brea wasn't sure what those were. "Sounds great!"

Brea sat in the living room and crossed her ankles beneath her. The space was decorated with simple sophistication and sharp lines that evoked Scandinavia. On the right-hand wall was a piece of art covered with a white sheet. "What's this?" Brea gestured toward the covered canvas. It wasn't exactly common for people not to reveal their decor.

"That's part of the reason I wanted you to come over," Neal said breezily, handing her the Negroni cocktail, a burnt-red drink in a square glass.

"Oh?" Brea's heart sank. She figured that now, Neal would beg her to ask Oriana to "deal" a piece of art he'd either made himself or come across. Ugh. She wasn't sure how to let him down easily.

But instead, Neal walked toward the artwork, counted to three, and pulled the sheet away to reveal the painting Oriana was currently selling to Walter Billington. The four-million-dollar painting.

Brea leaped from the couch, petrified, spilling her cocktail across her skirt. "What the heck is that?"

Neal laughed gently, clearly pleased with her reaction.

"I mean, Neal. What is that?" she repeated, trying to stabilize herself.

"Isn't it obvious? It's a replica of your four-million-dollar painting."

Brea sputtered. "A replica?"

"Isn't it perfect? I mean, it's exactly the same."

Brea walked toward it, flabbergasted. As far as she could tell, the painting was the same from every conceivable angle. And she should know. She'd spent many hours with the horrible thing, marveling at why it was worth so much.

Finally, she turned on her heel and gaped at Neal. "But why?"

Neal's smile was consistent, open. "Come on, Brea. I thought you were smart enough to figure it out by now."

Brea's stomach swam with fear. She hated being told she wasn't smart enough for something. Then again, she didn't want to name what was happening. It was horrific.

"Let me ask you a question. Why should Walter Billington spend four million dollars on that other painting when he could spend it on this replica— and never notice the difference?" Neal continued.

Brea thought she might throw up. Her mind whirred with the details of her friendship with Neal, trying to piece it together. *Had he followed her? Pinned her down? Manipulated her with his friendship?*

"The photographs?" she breathed. "When you spilled the beer, you must have..."

"Yes, I took one," Neal admitted with a wave of his hand. "I knew you wouldn't notice just one missing. And nobody else has at your little company, have they?"

Nobody had mentioned it. The painting was sold by now; they were just waiting for Walter to return from Tokyo to pick it up.

"Listen to me," Neal went on. "If you make the switch, I will give you two million dollars."

Something cold and hard fell into the pit of Brea's stomach. She glared at Neal, her hands balled into fists, and said, "I would never do that. I couldn't."

Neal's smile never wavered. He took a step toward

her. "You wouldn't? Not even to save the love of your life?"

Brea's jaw dropped. *How did he know about Kenny?*

"You don't need to trouble yourself with the how and the why of all of this," Neal went on. "Suffice it to say, I know a lot more about you than you know about me, and we'll keep it that way for safety reasons. All I need from you is the keys to the castle, so to speak. You help me, and I'll set you up for the rest of your life. Mark my words."

Chapter Sixteen

Present Day

When their hug broke, Brea and Oriana stared at each other for a long time, neither willing to be the first to speak. It reminded Oriana of the first days of their friendship when they'd been nervous four-year-olds, unversed in the ways of socializing. They both intuitively knew they needed a friend to get through preschool. And they'd settled on one another — maybe because of the color of their lunch boxes, the dolls they'd played with, or how their mothers had styled their hair.

Finally, Brea sputtered. "How did you find me?"

Oriana shook her head, tears springing to her eyes. Her throat was too tight to lend any real understanding.

"You have traveled a very long way," Brea said finally. "Why don't we go inside? Here. Let me take your suitcase."

Oriana watched quietly as Brea handled her heavy

suitcase, easily maneuvering it through the sand, up the porch steps, and into her house. Just before the door closed, she waved hello to her next-door neighbor, a Thai woman, who waved back and peered at Oriana curiously.

Brea's little home was small, just big enough for a woman who lived alone and wanted for nothing. Brea placed her suitcase near the table as Oriana linked her fingers together, trying not to remember the exact moment she'd last seen Brea in the flesh, as it was too painful.

Finally, Oriana found something to say: "It's beautiful here."

"Isn't it?" Brea wrapped a gray curl around her ear. "Growing up in Martha's Vineyard, I barely even knew where Thailand was."

"How long have you been here?" Oriana asked.

Brea furrowed her brow. "It's difficult for me to make sense of time anymore."

"I know what you mean," Oriana said. "Now that I'm fifty, I feel like I've lived so many lives, and I'm not completely sure which one I'm currently in."

"Well said," Brea offered. "Although here in Thailand, it's always sunny and always so gosh-darn hot. Without seasons, I don't feel the passage of time and don't feel any older. Only the mirror is here to tell me that's happening." Brea's smile broke open, and she said, "Although you look spectacular."

Oriana shrugged, feeling foolish. "I put a lot of money into it. Hair dye. Botox. Expensive face creams. It's all a lie, really."

"No," Brea assured her. "It's called prevention. Lots of women try to stay looking as young as possible, and there's nothing wrong with that. Here, that doesn't exist. The women just age with no cosmetic help whatsoever.

"Oh, the women here think I'm so strange. Look at me — I'm a mysterious white woman living alone in a little house. And my Thai is abysmal, so I can only have conversations with people who speak English or other expats— most of whom have run away from something. Like me."

Oriana thought she might burst into tears. Just the way Brea spoke of her reality was heartbreaking in its honesty. But Brea had always been this way— very self-aware in ways Oriana had never been.

Perhaps due to shock, Oriana again lost track of herself and had nothing to say. Brea's smile waned, and she shifted uncomfortably.

"I don't have a spare bed," Brea said finally. "But if you want to nap in my bedroom, it's yours."

"Oh. No." Although Oriana was exhausted, she wasn't sure she would ever be able to sleep again. "But I'm sort of hungry. Have you eaten dinner yet?"

Brea explained there was a little restaurant just down the beach that tourists generally didn't know about as it wasn't listed on Google. "I think they try to keep it that way," Brea said as she led Oriana back outside and toward the sands.

Oriana and Brea walked about two feet apart, headed toward a relative shack, from which aromatic scents of umami and sizzling vegetables and meats flowed.

"That's better than any advertisement," Oriana breathed with her eyes closed.

"The food here is to die for," Brea agreed.

It was clear that they were both avoiding the real topic at hand: why Oriana had just flown halfway around the world. But as they sat at a picnic table overlooking the water, Oriana struggled to comprehend her reasoning. The woman she saw before her, the woman with open, honest eyes and long, flowing salt and pepper hair, clearly had nothing to do with this blackmailer.

Oriana and Brea both ordered Pad Thai and glasses of coconut water. As they sat quietly, they listened to the sound of the noodles sizzling in the skillet as the chef flipped them around. Oriana sipped her coconut water and exhaled all the air from her lungs.

"How's Reese?" Brea asked. "And Alexa and Joel?"

Gosh, Alexa and Joel had been just little things the last time Oriana and Brea had seen one another.

"Reese is the same," Oriana said quietly. "He's gotten into app development, which is a field I don't know anything about."

"But Reese was always getting into fields we knew nothing about," Brea remembered. "He's a genius."

"He seems to sense where the technological wave is headed next," Oriana said with a smile.

"I still haven't gotten a smartphone," Brea said. "And I don't think I would have gotten one if I'd stayed home. I mean, unless Reese had talked me into it, of course."

Oriana laughed, imagining this alternate timeline and trying not to feel too glum about it. "I hate my smartphone sometimes. I want to throw it out the window and go back to the old ways. Remember when we had to call each other on the party line?"

"What I remember better is eavesdropping on your neighbors," Brea said mischievously. "When your mom caught us, she was so angry!"

"At least until we told her the gossip we'd heard,"

Oriana remembered, blushing at the memory. Oh gosh. She missed her mother.

"And Alexa? Joel?"

Oriana explained that Alexa had a toddler, Benny, who'd just gone into cancer remission. Brea looked stricken, tugging her hair.

"A little boy like that should never go through so much pain," she breathed.

Oriana nodded, her heart in her throat. "We were just so happy when the doctor told us he was going to be all right."

"I can't even imagine. What a relief."

Before Oriana could say anything more, the chef dropped off their Pad Thai and silverware. Immediately, Brea stirred it with a fork to portion out all the toppings. Oriana did the same, imitating her. She wanted to look like she fit in, too.

The food was ridiculously delicious. Each bite was transcendent, a mixture of salt, umami, and peanut flavorings that came together in the wonderful texture of the noodles.

"You can't get Thai food like this in the States," Oriana said.

"I imagine not," Brea said. "We're in Thailand, after all. It doesn't get much better than this."

Oriana laughed. "There was that Thai restaurant in Greenwich Village, remember? We used to go there sometimes for lunch."

"I remember. We thought it was killer."

"But it wasn't as good as this," Oriana affirmed. "Even though the chef was from Chiang Mai."

Brea leaned back in her chair. "I can't believe you remember that."

"I remember so much from our years in New York," Oriana offered quietly.

"You crammed a lot of living into those years," Brea said. "You had two small children, a huge career, and so many clients to look after. Plus, you and Reese were still one of the happiest couples I knew in the city."

Oriana slid her tongue over her teeth, unsure how to respond. Brea, too, had crammed a lot of life into those years— but the life hadn't been happy. Oriana knew that now.

Suddenly, Oriana couldn't take it anymore. Despite eating half her meal, she set down her fork, tapped her napkin over her mouth, and whispered, "I have a problem, Brea."

Brea furrowed her brow and set down her fork, as well. Off to the side, the chef looked at them, his face marred with worry, thinking they didn't like the food. Oriana couldn't care about him right now.

"I have been receiving very strange messages," Oriana whispered under her breath, despite them being the only people at the restaurant right now besides the chef. "The first one just said, 'I know what you did in 1998.'"

Brea's jaw dropped. Leaning forward, she whispered, "And you have no idea who sent it to you?"

"No. And that wasn't the only one," Oriana went on. "I've been living in a state of perpetual panic for weeks. And I can't take it anymore."

Brea nodded and crossed her arms over her chest. She looked at a loss. Strangely, Oriana felt herself breathing easier, if only because it was nice not to carry this on her own.

"So, I guess I just want to ask, who else knows about

this?" Oriana asked. "Who could possibly be blackmailing me?"

Brea blinked several times. "Neal is dead."

"But Neal must have worked with someone," Oriana pushed it.

"He painted it himself," Brea said quietly. "He didn't want it to be messy."

"But he must have sold it to someone."

"I don't know who he sold it to," Brea said. "But whoever it was, they have so much money that they don't need to blackmail you. Besides. I doubt they know your involvement in the situation at all."

Oriana's stomach stirred with panic. None of it was adding up.

"And Walter never figured it out?" Brea asked.

Oriana shook her head, dreading the idea that someday, perhaps soon, Walter would learn of how Oriana had wronged him all those years ago. They'd been friends for twenty-five years at this point. Twenty-five years, built on her lie.

"And you can't think of anyone else who could be blackmailing me?" Oriana asked.

"I wish I could," Brea offered sadly. "I've had no contact with anyone since I left. And I've wanted it that way." Brea lifted her fork again, glancing at the chef, who breathed a sigh of relief. In Thai, Brea said something to him, and then he turned back around, leaving them alone.

"What did you say?" Oriana asked, impressed with Brea's language skills.

"I told him we love the food," Brea said. "He felt insulted because we weren't eating quickly enough."

Oriana laughed gently, although, on the inside, she

felt busted up, broken. She wasn't sure she would be able to eat the rest of her meal.

Slowly, Brea wrapped her fork with noodles and ate, chewing thoughtfully. Oriana forced herself to do the same.

"Brea?" Oriana whispered, hardly daring to ask what she wanted to ask.

Brea looked at her.

"Did you ever, you know, get together with anyone out here?" Oriana wanted to ask: *have you been alone this whole time?* But the words were crass and terrible.

"I haven't met anyone, naw," Brea answered. "It's sort of hard to get to know anyone when you spend all your time running from yourself, you know?"

Oriana nodded, more broken-hearted than ever. All this time, Oriana had been allowed to live a wonderful, love-filled life. Meanwhile, Brea had been on the run.

After dinner, as they walked along the beach back toward Brea's little house, Oriana confessed she was exhausted.

"You must be so jet-lagged," Brea said. "I remember when I first got out here. I slept for three days." She paused, then added, "Of course, that happens to me sometimes. I just pass out and don't wake up for a while."

Oriana knew that was a symptom of depression. She wondered if Brea had ever sought medical help but decided it wasn't her place to ask. Not now.

Back at Brea's place, she insisted on making up the bed and giving it to Oriana. Oriana fought long and hard against it, but mid-yawn, she burst into a mix of laughter and tears and recognized she couldn't fight a moment more.

"You can have the other side," Oriana said as she

slipped into Brea's bed, her eyes half-closed. "It's not like we haven't shared a bed a million times before."

Brea's voice was sweet yet resigned. "We're old ladies now. We need our space."

This was the last Oriana heard before her world faded to black, and she was allowed, mercifully, to sleep.

Chapter Seventeen

November 1998

Kenny's kidney transplant was scheduled for two days before Thanksgiving. The morning of, Brea got out of bed before five to drink coffee and worry herself silly at the kitchen counter. It would be a day for the ages, one she would never forget in all her life. And gosh. She just wanted it to be over already.

When Brea had announced her "job raise" to Kenny and Valerie, she'd also explained to Valerie (with brand-new confidence) that she and Kenny needed their apartment to themselves again. "You can stay in the city. I'll help you pay for a room," Brea had explained. Valerie had jumped at it, with Brea assuring her it was only temporary. "As soon as Kenny gets well again, we won't need any more help," she'd said as sweetly as she could. She'd also said that Valerie wasn't allowed at the hospital on the day of Kenny's surgery, which Valerie had begrudgingly agreed to. Brea thought if Valerie was with her at the hospital, her head might explode.

When Kenny awoke a little while later, Brea helped him get up, shower, and dress. He was terribly weak, his arms and legs like putty, but he cracked jokes with her and made her smile in a way that nearly reminded her of the "old" Kenny. This did little to distract Brea from her horrific fears. Not everyone survived kidney transplants. Not everyone woke up on the other side.

Brea had asked for the day off from work, explaining to Oriana that Kenny's mother was in town, and they wanted to show her the sights. "Oh no. I know how much you don't like Valerie," Oriana had said, wrinkling her nose. "Let me know if you need backup. I can swoop in at any time to help out. I've got plenty of gossip to throw at her!" Brea had laughed, thinking it was incredible that she'd managed to lie so often to her best friend over the past couple of months. It made her feel disconnected from her heart.

At the hospital, Brea and Kenny sat in the waiting room, holding hands. Brea tried to think of something to say, anything to get Kenny's mind off his worries, but she was too tormented with her own.

Just before they called Kenny in, though, Brea made eye contact with him and said, "You're the love of my life, you know that?"

Kenny's eyes glinted with tears. "I know. You're mine, too. But that goes without saying, doesn't it?"

Brea laughed gently. "You think I'm being overly dramatic, don't you?"

"As usual," Kenny joked.

Brea chuckled, allowing tears to flow. She kissed him with her eyes closed, thinking he was the only man she'd ever kissed— and she was just fine with that. She'd never wanted anyone else.

After they wheeled Kenny back into surgery, Brea sat in the waiting room for a long time, staring out the window at the city, which made her feel out of her element. Around her, very sick people streamed in and out, most of them in wheelchairs, some of them at the end of their lives. Their fear or resignation made Brea sick to her stomach, and she stood up to pace outside, shivering in the November chill. Everything was decorated for Christmas. Wreaths hung on doors, garlands wrapped around telephone poles, and Christmas songs spat out of speakers. She couldn't imagine feeling any Christmas cheer.

At the stoplight, she paused for a moment, stared down at the pavement, and considered what she'd done. She'd stolen the keys to the gallery from Oriana's desk, then led Neal inside to swap out the painting. She'd taken the money and watched Neal slip into a taxi and disappear through the night.

Now, she had nearly two million dollars in bills under a floorboard in the apartment she shared with Kenny. And he had absolutely no idea. Nobody did. In fact, she'd been in the gallery when Walter had come to bring the painting home. As Walter had paced like a cat in front of the painting, Brea's stomach had swirled with such anxiety that she'd thought she might die.

"It really is something," Walter had said finally before turning back to nod at two of his employees, who then set to work wrapping the painting to take it home. "Oriana, you've really outdone yourself. I've told all my dearest friends about your services. I hope this isn't the last time we see one another, in both an art context and a social one."

Oriana had smiled like a princess who'd just been told she'll be queen. After Walter had left, she'd taken Brea's hand in hers and squealed, "We did it! It's gone! The painting is gone!" What Oriana didn't know, of course, was that the painting had been gone for three days at that point.

During the hours Brea waited for Kenny's surgery to finish, Brea worked herself up to such a panic that often, she wasn't sure she could breathe. Now that Neal had gotten the painting out of her, he'd stopped all forms of communication. She suspected he didn't even live in the apartment he'd invited her to— that it had all been a ruse. Probably, Neal wasn't even his real name.

Oh gosh. And what if Kenny didn't make it through the surgery? What would Brea do? She'd put her and Oriana's careers on the line for Neal and his cash, all for Kenny's health. And if it didn't work out? Where would she be, then?

There was no life after Kenny, Brea knew. She wouldn't be able to pursue a career. She couldn't pretend to be anything short of a very lonely, crazy woman.

When Brea started shaking uncontrollably in the hospital's waiting room, one of the nurses approached her with a glass of juice.

"You okay, honey?" The woman was quite a bit older than Brea. She probably saw women like her freaking out in the waiting room ten times a week.

Brea sipped her juice but was unable to stabilize herself.

"Is there anyone you can call to be here with you?" the nurse asked. "Anyone? A colleague? A neighbor?"

Brea closed her eyes. In the darkness was a single face — and that face was Oriana's. She was the only friend she'd truly ever known besides Kenny. And although she wasn't thinking clearly, as she was so heavy with guilt and a feeling of loss, she felt sure she needed to tell Oriana about the surgery. It was finally time.

Brea ambled to the telephone to ring the office, but the office secretary said Oriana had gone home for the day. Although this was strange for Oriana, it wasn't unheard of, especially this close to the holidays. Oriana had pledged to have a fun-filled Thanksgiving weekend with her family.

Reese answered the phone on the third ring. "Hello? Reese Jenkins speaking."

"Reese?" Brea's voice sounded so small.

"Is that Brea?" Reese was boisterous now. "Oriana's right here. You want to talk to her?"

"Very much."

A moment later, Oriana got on the phone, sounding vibrant and confident. "Is it time for me to swing in and distract Kenny's mother from tormenting you?"

Suddenly, Brea burst into loud, messy tears. It was all too much: the lying, Kenny's sickness, and her disconnect from her friend. She couldn't stand it anymore.

"Brea? What's wrong?" Oriana was stricken. "Tell me where you are! I'll come to you."

Brea blubbered. "I'm at the hospital."

"What? Oh my God!" Oriana was appropriately panicked. "Was there an accident? Is Kenny all right?"

Brea took a deep breath. "Kenny's in surgery. Will you please come? I need you."

"Which department?" Oriana demanded. "I'm on my way."

Oriana was exceedingly good— a good friend, a good businesswoman, a good wife, and a good mother. Perhaps this was part of the reason Brea had come to resent her, even though she loved her so much. She just couldn't keep up with her goodness, especially now that she'd done the worst thing of all in stealing from her.

Oh, it was terrible.

But when Oriana arrived twenty-five minutes later to take Brea in her arms, Brea decided, if only for a moment, to forget her resentment and cry on Oriana's shoulder. After a little while, Brea was able to explain that Kenny had been sick for a while and that he'd finally been able to secure a kidney transplant surgery. "But he might not get well. It's never a sure thing," she finished, blubbering.

"Brea," Oriana whispered. "It's going to be okay! This hospital is wonderful. I've had several clients tell me so themselves. And people recover from kidney transplants all the time! It's more common than you think. Now. Can you take a deep breath for me? In and out. In and out."

Brea closed her eyes and followed Oriana's breathing instructions, filling her lungs and exhaling as much as she could. *Why had she gotten so lucky with Oriana's friend-ship? Why had she ever doubted it? Maybe she should have just asked Oriana for the money, somehow?* It would have been better than what she'd done.

Oh gosh! She'd probably single-handedly destroyed her best friend's career!

"When was the last time you ate anything?" Oriana asked.

"I have no idea," Brea answered.

"Why don't we go down the road and grab a bite?"

Brea felt reluctant, but the nurse explained it would

be quite a while before Brea was allowed into the room to see Kenny— at which time he would still be asleep.

"Kenny would want you to take care of yourself," Oriana assured her. "You two are getting married, remember? He wants you to be healthy and happy, just as you want him to be."

Brea nodded and allowed herself to be led up and out of the waiting room, down three blocks, to a Chinese restaurant with a buffet. Oriana explained that she hardly dared allow herself to go inside, as she adored every single thing they made— but that this was a special occasion. It called for greasy, messy Chinese food. It called for companionship over many, many calories.

And as they ate, often without words, Brea allowed herself to feel deeply grateful for this woman and all she'd done for her, ever since she'd walked up to her at age four and complimented the butterfly clip in her hair. *"I have one, too,"* Oriana had said.

Just like that, their friendship had been formed. And just like that, Brea had found a way to destroy it and build it on a lie. The guilt would ultimately find a way to kill her, she felt. But as long as Kenny was alive, she had to believe it was worth it.

Chapter Eighteen

Present Day

Oriana awoke on the island of Ko Tao at eight in the morning, bleary-eyed yet well-rested, with the Southeast Asian sunlight searing her bedsheets. She thought it was incredible how different the sunlight could be, depending on where on the earth's surface you viewed it— that it could be warm and orange or harsh and cold. She wondered if the kind of sunlight you were born looking at decided what sort of person you turned into.

Tenderly, she walked from Brea's bed to the hallway, thinking she would find Brea asleep on the couch or perhaps sipping coffee or preparing for her day— a day Oriana could hardly fathom as it had so little to do with the life they'd shared together. Instead, she found Brea wide awake, her spine straight, a suitcase by the door. She looked like she was heading to war.

"Brea? What are you doing?" Oriana leaned against the wall, crossing her arms over her chest.

Brea's jaw quivered. "You aren't going back to face this alone."

Oriana couldn't believe this. Here in Thailand, she'd expected to find answers about who was blackmailing her, and instead, she'd found the source of her problems— a woman so wrought with guilt that she'd abandoned Oriana, abandoned her life, and burrowed herself into a life without family, without friendships, for years and years, as a way to punish herself. Oriana had never wanted Brea to punish herself.

But perhaps, immediately after everything that had happened and she'd discovered the truth, Oriana hadn't been so open-hearted, so kind. Perhaps Oriana had said something that had pushed Brea across the world.

No regrets could change the past.

"You don't have to do this, Brea," Oriana said, walking toward the kitchen table and collapsing into a chair. "It's not your battle anymore. I just thought that maybe you could help. And it's okay that you can't."

"I started this," Brea told her. "I intend to finish it. I want to be there when the ax falls. And I want it to fall on my neck."

Oriana groaned and rubbed her neck, unsure if she liked all these analogies. "Brea, come on. You haven't been in the States in how long?"

"I have a passport that will work for me," Brea explained. "It's not my name, per se. But it's a name that doesn't ring any alarm bells."

Oriana groaned again. "You really went all out on the hiding aspect."

Brea cocked her head. "I still can't figure out how you found me."

"I paid someone a lot of money," Oriana said with a shrug. "It always comes down to that."

Brea grimaced. "I guess you're right."

Oriana and Brea regarded one another, both lost in the chaos of the past. Finally, Oriana stood back up and set to work, brewing them a pot of coffee. "I can't think yet. Just give me a little bit of time." As the coffee dripped into the pot, she turned her attention back to Brea. "You would really come back? Right now? With me?"

Brea raised her left shoulder. "The fact that you came all the way here just to see me means a lot."

"But I didn't. I came here because I thought—"

"Because you thought I knew who was messing with your career. I know," Brea said. "But you could have sent someone else. You could have sent a lawyer. That's how these things normally go." She shook her head. "Instead, you came yourself."

"I had to be discrete."

"You're still the person I think of the most," Brea said, ignoring her. "The one I feel the most regretful about leaving behind. I know that's ironic since you're the one I hurt the most, too."

Oriana blinked back tears. How could she explain to Brea how much this meant to her? How much she'd ached for Brea to be there during so many eras of her life. She'd missed her daughter and son growing up. She'd missed the birth of her three grandchildren. She'd missed so many Christmases, Fourth of Julys, sailing adventures, and on and on.

But still, Oriana's love for Brea was strong, regardless of what she'd done.

"You got away with it," Oriana breathed. "For so long,

I thought nobody knew. But somebody must have figured it out."

"I just don't know who," Brea said.

Oriana poured them both mugs of coffee, and together they sat out in the thick heat of the back porch, sipping, watching the island awaken around them. The ocean seemed mystical, far more turquoise than anything back home, and Brea explained quietly that it was almost like bath water, that swimming in it reminded her less of the Atlantic than the Katama Lodge and Wellness Spa.

"Do you want to get in?" Brea asked nervously.

Oriana cocked her head, remembering how Rita had told her to pack a swimsuit, that she'd thrust her hand into her drawer and come up with a black bikini, a yellow one-piece. She couldn't remember the last time she'd worn a swimsuit in public— let alone halfway around the world. She hadn't even been able to verbalize her fears about her body to Reese, but now she heard herself say, "I feel so weird in a swimsuit now that I'm fifty."

Brea nodded. "I feel like my body is abandoning me. The more I try to work with it, the more it works against me."

Oriana wanted to cry again. This was the sort of conversation they should have been having for years— one that discussed every single era of getting older, from the twenties, through the forties, through menopause.

"Do you think it ever gets easier?" Oriana asked with a laugh.

Brea shook her head. "No, but I think it's good to embrace the swimsuit. Our bodies are a sign of the years we've lived, ones we need to embrace and be proud of. If anything, we should be grateful."

Thirty minutes later, Brea and Oriana were at the

beach, wearing big t-shirts and shorts over their swim-suits. For a mile on either side of the white, sandy beach were no people, no tourists, and the palm trees around them shifted gently to and fro, majestic beasts beneath the shimmering blue. Oriana closed her eyes and listened to the subtle sweep of the water. And then, Brea's hand found hers as Brea whispered, "Want to go in on three?"

This was what they'd done all those years ago when the ocean had terrified Oriana. She'd been so young, so little, armed with only a few weeks of swimming lessons. The ocean had been so sinister, this mass filled with sharks, whales, jellyfish, and mysterious sunken ships. But Brea had been unafraid, which had astounded Oriana. They'd probably been eight years old.

After they removed their t-shirts and shorts to reveal Oriana's black two-piece and Brea's blue tankini, Oriana tried to resist speaking ill of herself in her head. This was the body that had birthed two babies, the body that had brought her through time. She'd fed this body well. It had taken her on six-mile runs and on long walks through Central Park. This was the body that had loved Reese in innumerable ways, that had climbed mountainsides and skied down slopes.

"All right. On three. One, two, three," Oriana said, and together, the two fifty-year-old women burst toward the blue, splashing through the very warm water until they got in up to their waists. Oriana laughed, amazed at how alike the water was to the air over them. It was seamless.

Brea shifted back to float on the water, her dark salt and pepper hair spreading out on the top of the water. Oriana could have cried at how beautiful she looked.

It was then that she allowed herself to ask the question that had been heavily on her mind for many years.

"Why didn't you tell me?"

Brea's eyes shifted toward her. "Tell you what?"

Oriana swallowed. "Why didn't you tell me Kenny was so sick?"

Truthfully, that was probably the thing that stung the most.

"You were my best friend," Oriana went on. "But Kenny was a dear friend to me and Reese. We should have known about it. We should have been there to take care of you both."

Brea stood in the water, so her hair was flat across her chest and upper stomach. Her eyes were enormous. "I wanted to tell you. I just didn't know how. That probably sounds crazy to you, so many years afterward. Because in our memories, we were always thick as thieves, weren't we?"

"I like to think we were," Oriana breathed.

"But I felt you falling away from me," Brea offered. "I was so proud of you, the person you already were and the person you were going to be. But I felt like there was a shield around you."

Oriana frowned. In her memory, she'd been a loyal friend to Brea, attempting to give her a leg-up in an industry Brea wasn't quite ready for. But then again, the industry was cut-throat in ways that had nearly swallowed Oriana whole. During those early years, Oriana had had to push herself, if only to keep herself above water, metaphorically.

"I'm going to come with you," Brea told Oriana again, her eyes heavy. "I've been away for too long. And I think, if you left me here alone to go back, my heart might break so much that it'll stop beating. And I'll just get older and older, without a heart."

Oriana nodded, sensing Brea was right— that, now they were back together, they had to face this head-on.

"When this comes out," Oriana offered, "we have to stand strong."

"We will," Brea said.

"But we'll do it on Martha's Vineyard. Where we've always belonged," Oriana finished.

Back at Brea's house, Oriana purchased two flights back to Boston to leave the following afternoon. This gave Brea just a few hours to tell her landlord she was leaving and pack up her few things.

"People do this kind of thing in Thailand all the time," Brea explained. "They just take off. We're all running away from something. But now, I'm running toward my past. How funny is that."

Chapter Nineteen

June 2000

The weather on Martha's Vineyard hadn't cooperated all June long. Tourists were miserable, cooped up in hotel rooms as a violent rain splattered across their windowpanes, and sailors protested, going south to the Caribbean to have the summers they'd dreamed for.

But alas, Brea and Kenny had booked their wedding for the third weekend in June. And there was nowhere in the world they'd rather have the occasion, even if Martha's Vineyard was rain-soaked.

On the morning of the wedding, Brea awoke in her house, in the bed she normally shared with Kenny. The skies were gray, as usual, and there was a patter of rain atop the twittering of birds. Beside her in bed, a blond woman sighed and flipped over, then smiled sleepily.

"Brea, darling! It's your wedding day!"

Brea laughed and sat up in bed, her hair tousled. Last night after the rehearsal dinner, her bridal party had returned to her home— Oriana and a few other friends from high school and college. Together, they'd stayed up past midnight, laughing together as another storm passed through the night sky.

"Oh gosh. I'm hungover," Oriana groaned, rubbing her eyes. "Are you?"

Brea was surprised to say she wasn't. Perhaps due to nerves, she'd kept her drinking to a minimum, feeling fizzy on love, conversation, and laughter.

"I'll make coffee," Brea assured her best friend and maid of honor. "You'll be better in no time."

"I hope you're right!"

Brea hurried down the staircase of the Victorian home she and Kenny had purchased six months ago when Brea and Oriana had decided it was time to take their art dealing back to Martha's Vineyard. They'd had enough of the city. Oriana had a hefty client base and plenty of contacts, and even Brea had cultivated a client list of her own— one that most art dealers coveted. New Yorkers had begun to call them the "dynamic duo" of the art world.

In the kitchen, the coffee bubbled and spat into the pot, and Oriana collapsed at the kitchen counter and rubbed her temples. Despite the alcohol, she looked bright and beautiful, her skin shining.

"I still can't believe you and Kenny bought this old place," she said, eyeing the beautiful kitchen, the big bay windows that looked out across the water, and the living room featuring a baby grand piano. "I mean, don't you remember walking past it as kids? We always prayed one of us would end up here. And you did!"

"Your place isn't half-bad, either," Brea reminded her.

Oriana's place was three times the size of Kenny and Brea's, something both of them knew. What Oriana didn't know, of course, was that part of what Brea had earned through Neal for switching the forged painting had gone into this place's purchase. This had been essential, as Brea's client list wasn't comparable to Oriana's— not yet, anyway.

Still, for whatever reason, Oriana hadn't questioned it, as though to her, everyone had just enough money to go around.

Brea poured them both mugs of coffee, and together, they sat out on the back porch and watched the rain patter across the pavement and lush grass. The air was clean and crisp, and the coffee was hazelnut and warm, and Brea wasn't sure if she'd ever been half as happy as this. Everything had fallen into place. And best of all, Oriana had never caught on to her scheme. Perhaps her lie would go on forever. Perhaps Brea would be able to convince herself that it had never been a lie, that she'd never made the switch in the first place.

People convinced themselves of lies all the time.

Not long afterward, the other bridesmaids awoke. Oriana and Brea busied themselves with making eggs, turkey sausages, and biscuits for breakfast, plus slicing some strawberries and brewing more coffee. Brea allowed herself to drown in the beautiful voices of the women she loved the most.

A few hours later, Brea, Oriana, and the other bridesmaids got ready in a little room at the church, stepping into dresses and buttoning one another up. In the mirror, Brea saw the portrait of a young and beautiful bride with an iconic dress with artistic flair, a long skirt, and a sleek off-the-shoulder top. It was a dress fit for the kind of artist she wanted to grow to be.

"You look stunning," Oriana said from behind her, smiling with tears in her eyes. "I can't believe my favorite couple is finally getting married."

Brea walked down the aisle to marry Kenny, the love of her life, the only man with whom she wanted to have children and grow old with. Kenny had gained back all the weight since his surgery in late 1998; his hair was glossy and wild, and his eyes were alight and filled with optimism. As they held one another's gaze, Brea swam in memories of their many years together, of all the trials and hardships they'd been through. She tried not to remember what she'd done and stolen, all in the name of his health. But when she found herself thinking of it, a single voice in her mind told her to look at what good it had done! *He's alive! Who cares about that stupid painting?*

A pastor asked them to say their vows, and with their family and friends as their witnesses, Brea and Kenny pledged their love and their lives. And afterward, they kissed, with Kenny dipping her down low and lifting her back up again as the crowd went wild.

Because the rain just wouldn't quit, Brea's family set up a huge circus tent, beneath which they'd placed twenty round tables with eight chairs at each. Kenny and Brea sat at a long table at one end of the tent, with Reese and Oriana on either side of them. One after another, Oriana and Reese made speeches, honoring their long friendship and looking forward to many more years.

"Kenny, you've been through a lot, my man," Reese

said into the microphone. "And we're just so dang glad you're healthy, with your best girl by your side. Looking forward to many more years with you. Life wouldn't be the same without you."

For dinner, they ate seafood— trout and sea bass and clam chowder, potatoes, roasted vegetables, and Kenny's favorite, macaroni and cheese. Brea had laughed at that choice, saying, "Regular people don't have macaroni and cheese at weddings! Do they?" And to this, Kenny had reminded her, "We're not regular people, baby."

And it was true. For together, they'd beaten death. That wasn't regular in the slightest.

A couple of hours later, as the music pumped from the speakers, family members whirled around in shining shoes, and people attacked second servings of cake, Oriana walked across the dance floor to loop her arm through Brea's. Kenny was busy with Reese, laughing about something with their arms thrown across one another's shoulders and beers in their hands.

"So! Tell me," Oriana said mischievously. "When can I expect cousins for my kids?"

"You were never very patient, Oriana Coleman. You know that?"

"I've been told my impatience is one of my best attributes," Oriana joked. "It means I get things done."

"You know I've wanted kids for years," Brea said softly, tucking a curl behind her ear. "We just couldn't afford them back in the city. And then, with Kenny's illness, time just got away from us. But we're still young! We could have five kids, even."

"Why stop at five when you could have eight?" Oriana quipped.

"After seeing what you went through with your children back in the city," Brea began, "I don't think I could handle the stress of that."

"Yes, but we're out on our own now," Oriana reminded her. "It's just us, our client list, and all the art to deal in the world. Which means if you need to take time off to care for your children, be my guest. We aren't in the cut-throat world of New York City anymore. We need to be there for each other."

As Oriana said this, another wave of guilt came over Brea, and she crossed her arms over her chest.

"What's wrong?" Oriana demanded.

"Oh! Nothing. I just can't believe it's almost over," Brea said, gesturing across the dance floor.

"It is sad, isn't it? I dreamed of my wedding my entire childhood, and then whoosh, it was done." Oriana shook her head. "But there's so much more to look forward to. Don't you think?"

Although it was common practice to stay in a honey-moon suite immediately after the reception— for brides and grooms supposedly craved beautiful, fancy things, Brea and Kenny had decided that there was no place like home for them. A sober driver dropped them off around one in the morning, and they scurried through the rain and stood on the back porch, waving goodbye. There, Kenny kissed Brea delicately and rubbed her shoulders.

"So. I'm your husband now," he said, his tone lilting.

"I heard something about that," Brea joked. "Does that mean you'll take the trash out for the rest of our lives?"

"You always were a romantic, Brea," Kenny said.

"I know. My head is in the clouds." Brea laughed and rose onto her tiptoes to kiss him, her heart pumping hard.

Kenny and Brea's marriage was blissful, starting from

that very first day. Often, they woke up earlier than they needed to, just to sit at the kitchen table with cups of coffee as the light of the morning streamed through the windows, talking about whatever was on their minds. It was bizarre, perhaps, that although they'd known one another since their early teenage years, they never ran out of things to say.

Kenny started a new job as head chef at a French seafood restaurant in Edgartown, and Brea found herself up to her ears with new clients in the business she and Oriana had started together— The Martha's Vineyard Art Club. Eventually, they dreamed of hiring people to work under them, but for now, it was just the two of them meeting with clients, driving to New York, researching new artists, and celebrating their triumphant rise through the art world, despite their decision to leave the big city.

"Alexa and Joel are flourishing," Oriana said once as they drove back from New York to Martha's Vineyard. "I can't imagine what kind of people they would have been had we stayed in the city. Nothing against lifelong New Yorkers, of course. But I feel that our particular brand of Martha's Vineyard love is so powerful— nothing I want to deny my children."

Brea understood what she meant. And, just as they'd planned, she and Kenny were trying for a baby, with the hope to welcome him or her by the following year. Every time Brea walked past the spare bedroom upstairs, she daydreamed that their baby was already in there, fast asleep in a crib. But unfortunately, Brea was met with disappointment every month and the growing belief that maybe something was wrong with her.

"We'll go to the doctor soon," Kenny assured her. "But right now, aren't we having a great time on our own?"

Brea had to admit he was right. Without children, they were untethered, apt to take off for spontaneous vacations whenever their hearts craved it. They flew to Paris, went to California, and ate Cajun food in Louisiana. They went sailing, hiking, and snorkeling and discussed a trip to South America to see Machu Picchu.

Brea had a hunch that because Kenny had thought he would die, he now wanted to live as wildly and freely as he could. That didn't negate his desire for children; he just didn't see the rush. Brea tried to take a deep breath, to calm herself down, and to remember that sometimes, people had babies later in life. There was no pressure besides the one you put on yourself.

But toward the end of the year, just a week or so before Christmas, everything changed. Brea had been at the office with Oriana, going over their next year's goals and strategies. The plan was to return home, change, pick up Kenny, and head to a party with Oriana and Reese. Snow flurries swirled across her car window, and a slick ice forced her to drive slowly, carefully. Once she parked in the driveway, she breathed a sigh of relief, stepped out of the car, walked carefully to the front door, opened it, and discovered, with a horrible jolt in her gut, that Kenny had collapsed on the living room floor.

"Kenny!" Brea left the door open and scrambled to sit next to him. Although he was still breathing, his skin was clammy and cold. "Oh my gosh. I'm going to call an ambulance, Kenny, okay? But I'm right here, baby. I'm right here."

The ambulance arrived fifteen minutes later. As she waited, Brea held Kenny's hand delicately as tears streamed down her cheeks. Because she didn't know what else to do, she narrated their future to Kenny, telling him about the trips they would go on, and the children they would have. His eyes still glinted with life, but even though she'd covered him with blankets, his skin continued to chill.

Up at the hospital, Brea paced nervously, thinking she was in a nightmare, one she would surely wake up from. This was why she didn't reach out to anyone and didn't call Oriana or Kenny's family. This was why she was alone when the doctor came out to tell her that Kenny hadn't made it. This was why she was alone when she fell to her knees and realized her life, as she'd once known it, was officially over. In many ways, her life had ended the day Kenny received his diagnosis in 1998— but they'd been allowed two extra years to say goodbye. It had been a blessing, maybe, but also a terrible curse.

Chapter Twenty

Despite fear for what awaited them at the end of the journey, the flight back to the United States was a gorgeous experience. Throughout, Oriana and Brea sat side-by-side in business class, sipping cocktails, chatting, or watching television, happy to pretend that the rest of the world would leave them alone, that the blackmailer would grow tired of his blackmailing, that Brea could return to Martha's Vineyard unscathed by the terrible events of the past.

"You have got to try this sundae," Oriana insisted, moaning as she took another spoonful.

Brea blushed and dug her spoon into the ice cream, making sure to get a small piece of chocolate brownie and a bit of caramel. She closed her eyes as she ate and said, "It's good, but it isn't as good as that place we went to growing up."

"Ray's? Oh my gosh. I can't believe I forgot about that."

"We used to beg your dad to take us, remember?" Brea's eyes widened.

"He blamed us for his weight gain that summer," Oriana said with a laugh. "But he always ordered an extra scoop of ice cream."

"I guess two nine-year-old girls aren't great influences," Brea offered.

Across the aisle from them sat an older woman with slight shoulders and a wide-brimmed black hat. Oriana had been surprised that she'd left it on throughout the entire flight. Now, she smiled at Oriana and Brea, saying, "I hope you don't mind me interrupting, but it's so rare and lovely to overhear women such as yourselves. You've clearly had a wonderful, lifelong friendship. Many of my friends abandoned their female friends after marriage and children, which was sad to see."

Brea and Oriana exchanged timid glances. While this woman saw two fifty-year-old best friends, the truth was far more complicated.

"Just count yourselves lucky that you put one another first," the woman went on. "It's truly a gift."

When the plane touched down, it was three in the afternoon, Boston time, which made it three in the morning, Thailand time. Because Oriana's trip had been so brief, her body felt twisted and strange, like a pretzel. Brea constantly yawned as they moved through customs, her eyes dancing around the large room.

"When was the last time you were in America?" Oriana asked.

Brea winced. "I haven't been back since I left. I was just thinking that it has probably changed so much over the years."

162

"You'll have to tell me what you notice," Oriana said. "What's changed, and what feels the same."

"America has seemed like a dream to me all these years," Brea offered, blinking back tears. "I can't tell you how often I've woken up and wished that the Indian Ocean was the Atlantic. That the delicious Thai food I was eating was actually clam chowder. For so long, I've been living in 'paradise.' But all I wanted was to come back home. I just didn't know how."

Oriana's heart lifted. She knew Brea would never have had the strength to come back had it not been for Oriana going to get her.

She should have done that years ago.

Once in the parking garage, Brea ogled the vehicles, which looked remarkably different since 2000.

"Everything is so much bigger than I remember it," she whispered as she stepped into Oriana's car and buckled herself in. "In Thailand, I've driven nothing but a motorbike for years."

"Do you remember how to drive a car?" Oriana joked.

But Brea gave her an ominous look. "Truthfully, I'm slightly scared to try."

"You can take it slow," Oriana offered. "One thing at a time."

Brea grimaced. "Thank you."

As Oriana drove from the Boston airport to Woods Hole, where the ferry disembarked for Martha's Vineyard, she was amazed to see the "new world" through Brea's eyes. Brea clicked through radio stations, bouncing her head to songs she'd never heard before— even ones that were nearly twenty years old.

"What music were you into when you left?" Oriana asked, trying to remember.

"We both loved Sheryl Crowe, remember?" Brea said. "And Shania, of course. Kenny adored grunge music, but I could never get into it." She paused, then asked, "Is that still big?"

"Not really," Oriana said. "Although, now that I'm fifty, I can't say I'm hip with the times."

"You know more than me," Brea said. "I've kept a wide berth from the real world. And right now, listening to all this new music and seeing all these new things, I sort of feel like I'm on another planet."

"I can hardly imagine."

Oriana parked the car on the bottom level of the ferry, and together, the two friends struck out for the top deck, as Brea wanted to watch the island grow bigger on the horizon line. As Brea leaned against the railing, she whispered, "Do you remember the first time our parents let us leave the island on our own? We must have been seventeen."

Oriana did remember. They'd driven to Boston for a "girls' trip," but Chuck had demanded that they return to the Vineyard by nightfall. They'd spent the entire day running through second-hand clothing stores, eating delicious and greasy food, downing milkshakes, and pretending they were much older than they were— college-aged students with hardly any obligations, a little apartment in the city somewhere with their whole lives ahead of them. Once, a very scary older man approached them and asked them for directions in a way that creeped them out, and Brea and Oriana ran away from him, realizing they weren't as brave as they'd thought they were.

"We thought we were something special," Oriana said.

"I remember when we were on the ferry, returning

after our big day in Boston," Brea went on. "I felt almost the same on the ferry that day as I do today. The eight hours we spent alone on the island felt like a lifetime. They changed me, in a way."

Oriana was amazed at the comparison, yet she understood what Brea meant. Every day as a teenager had been filled with innumerable possibilities, which ultimately died off as they'd gotten older.

This late in September on Martha's Vineyard, the trees had begun to transform, greens bleeding into reds, oranges, and yellows, and leaves splintering from branches and falling to the ground. Still, the sky above was eggshell blue, and the temperature was rather warm in the upper sixties. As they drove slowly from the ferry, Brea was enraptured, leaning forward, trying to take it all in.

"You know what, Oriana?" Brea breathed. "It doesn't look so different from my dreams!"

Oriana laughed, blinking back tears. As she pulled up at a stoplight, she glanced at Brea, realizing they hadn't planned for their arrival. Oriana hadn't even told Reese about her reunion with Brea, nor why she'd gone to Thailand in the first place. She was no closer to discovering what was going on with the blackmailer than she'd been before that flight to Thailand.

But suddenly, Brea figured out the next step for both of them.

"Could you take me to the flower shop? And then to the cemetery?" Her voice wavered. "It's time I go see him."

Brea asked that Oriana remain in the car while she bought flowers. Oriana sensed this was because Oriana was recognizable across the island. Everyone had watched her grow up and knew her through and through. Brea, being twenty-three years older than she'd been the last time she'd stood on Vineyard soil, could fly under the radar a bit better.

Brea returned with a large bouquet of Black-eyed Susan's and Morning Glories, her eyes glistening with pride. On the drive to the cemetery, she remained quiet, her chin raised and her cheeks streaked with tears. Oriana tried to put herself in Brea's shoes, to imagine what it had been like to bury her husband so many years ago, then leave the only home you'd ever known immediately after. Brea had been floating, a boat without an anchor.

"You can come with me," Brea said after they parked. Oriana reasoned she said it because she really needed company.

Despite the many years between visits, Brea knew exactly where to go. Twenty-seven rows down, thirty-three rows to the right. That was where the large grave-stone sat, upon which was carved:

KENNY BALLARD
A Loving Husband and Friend
1973-2000

Because Kenny's family had died, Reese and Oriana were the only people who brought flowers to the grave site. Admittedly, over the years, they'd gotten lazier with it, often letting months go by. Oriana wished she could explain that to Brea, to tell her that they still thought of him often. But it wasn't the time to talk about the ways she'd failed her friend.

Brea knelt in front of the grave to place the bouquet in front of it, then began talking quietly to Kenny. Several paces back, Oriana couldn't quite make out what she said.

Again, she was overwhelmed with memories of Brea and Kenny's wedding, a stormy day in June, so long after Kenny's transplant. It had seemed that their love would last forever. It had seemed they were in the clear.

Before they left, Brea kissed the gravestone softly, turned, and hugged Oriana with her eyes closed. She shuddered against Oriana for several minutes, her hair flipping with the September winds. Oriana wished she could take away her dear friend's pain. She wished she could carry it for her.

Brea didn't argue when Oriana suggested they drive back to her house. It was getting dark and cold, and they were both starving. On the way, Oriana texted Reese to ask him to order pizza, and Reese sent a celebratory GIF that made Oriana laugh. When she showed Brea the GIF, she shook her head, smiling, and said, "I see you two haven't changed at all." This warmed Oriana's heart.

Oriana sensed Brea's nerves as they walked through the garage to enter the kitchen door. The kitchen was simmering with smells of melted cheese, tomato sauce, and spicy cured meats, and laughter and conversation echoed.

"GRAMMA!" Benny swung around the corner and ran directly into Oriana's legs, making her wince. "Grandma's home!" He announced properly.

Reese bounded forward to hug Oriana, then dropped back, his eyes shadowed. "Hello," he said to Brea, who stood nervously behind Oriana.

"Hi, Reese," Brea said very quietly.

Reese's jaw dropped. Oriana watched his face contort through shock, fear, and finally, joy.

"BREA?" He raced toward her and hugged her,

moving much faster than Oriana had seen him in years. "This is a crazy surprise! What are you doing here?"

After the hug, Brea's eyes were thicker with tears than ever. Behind Reese, Alexa, Alan, and Nora peered at them with curiosity.

"Everyone, this is my best friend, Brea," Oriana announced, striding through the kitchen and gesturing for Brea to follow. "She was working in Thailand, so we met up and decided it was time for her to visit."

Reese remained flabbergasted. Alexa had been too young when Brea was around to remember her properly, but she opened her arms to her, asking her how the trip had gone. Brea then shook Nora and Alan's hands as Nora said, "You have the most beautiful hair! Alan, doesn't she?"

Brea blushed and touched her wild, gray, and black mane. "I probably look like a hippie."

"I'm old," Nora explained. "Maybe I was a little bit of a hippie back in my day."

Everyone laughed, even Brea, although her cheeks were red with embarrassment. It was too much attention at once.

"I think we'd better eat," Reese began, realizing the awkwardness. "Brea? You still a fan of sausage, green peppers, and onions?"

"I haven't changed that much," Brea joked, accepting the plate piled with pizza.

"Sit down!" Alexa urged, gesturing for her to take a place at the table.

"Still can't believe you were in Thailand, as well," Reese repeated, preparing a plate for Benny, then for Alexa, as Oriana filled a plate for Nora, Alan, then herself. "I mean, what are the chances?"

Brea laughed nervously. "It was crazy, wasn't it, Oriana?"

"What part of Thailand?" Reese asked. "Bangkok?"

Brea looked at Oriana with an expression only Oriana could decipher. She got the hint that it was better to lie right now until they figured everything out... if they could.

"Yup! Bangkok," Brea said. "That's where most of the artists in Thailand live."

Reese slid his fingers through his hair, shaking his head. "I can't tell you how good it is to see you, Brea. We've thought about you so much over the years."

Brea's cheeks were cherry red. A moment of silence passed, during which Oriana thought she might collapse.

"Everyone! The pizza is getting cold," Oriana finally managed, remembering she was the woman of the house, the leader. She had to ensure everyone was happy, safe, and well-fed.

Just then, the doorbell rang. Panic shot through Oriana, and she leaped for the door. It stood to reason that the blackmailer would pick now to reach out. Brea was back, and both women were in his line of fire. Didn't he want to play with his prey a little bit more before the main event?

But instead, when Oriana opened the door, she was surprised to find her half-brother, Grant standing before her. He wore a goofy grin and extended his arms.

"Oriana! That was a quick trip, wasn't it?"

Oriana gaped at him, surprised. After all, in reality, she and her half-brothers had only met once thus far, which put their relationship at a strange point. They didn't quite know one another yet were headed some-where— which meant something.

"Oh! Oriana. I forgot to mention Grant was stopping by," Reese said, running behind her.

Grant's eyes were curious, hurt. "I hope I'm not intruding."

"Not at all," Oriana hurried to say, although, in reality, he sort of was.

"Grant was on the Vineyard today to see Chuck," Reese added. "I figured you'd want him to stop by."

"I think you were on the plane when I reached out to Reese," Grant explained easily. "But please. Tell me if I'm intruding. I have no problems finding a restaurant. We can catch up some other time."

But sending her half-brother away wasn't in Oriana's nature, not even during this difficult time. "Please. Come in! I'm just jet-lagged. We have plenty of pizza, right, Reese?"

Alexa hurried to grab another chair for the table, and together, they crowded around, with Reese piling a plate high with slices of pepperoni and onion for Grant.

"Brea? This is my brother," Oriana said nervously. "Grant, this is my best friend, Brea."

Grant had no idea that Oriana hadn't seen her best friend since the year 2000. Smoothly, he stuck out his hand to shake Brea's, and Brea said, "Nice to meet you. Chuck's your father?"

"Indeed," Grant said.

"I practically grew up at Oriana's house as a child," Brea explained. "I just adored Chuck."

Grant's smile faltered slightly. Oriana knew this was because he didn't like thinking about his father here on the Vineyard when he should have been on Nantucket with him and Roland.

"This pizza looks great," Grant said, avoiding the topic.

Oriana sat between Brea and Reese, two of her favorite people in the world, and heard herself laugh as Benny slathered his face with cheese and red sauce. It was true that a toddler could bring even the strangest crowd together.

"I wish I could eat like that," Grant joked.

"Nobody is stopping you," Brea reminded him.

As everyone cackled at Brea's joke, Reese cleared his throat and asked Brea and Oriana what they'd gotten up to in Thailand and what their favorite meal had been. To this, Brea and Oriana talked at length about the Pad Thai they'd eaten during their first evening together.

"I don't know if I'll ever be able to eat Pad Thai in the United States again," Oriana complained. "It was transcendent."

After dinner, Nora and Alan returned home, Alexa and Reese cleaned up the plates, Alexa put Benny to bed, and Reese headed to his office for some late-night work. This left Oriana, Brea, and Grant at the table with a bottle of wine, Oriana's head whirring with fear, and her ears perked to hear a knock at the door. Since Grant's appearance, she'd felt that the blackmailer wasn't far behind. She couldn't shake it.

"I've never made it to Thailand," Grant said, swirling his wine in his glass. "How long were you there, Brea?"

"Years," Brea answered solemnly.

"Wow!" Grant said.

"And she hasn't been back to the States since 2000," Oriana said, which was a fact she still couldn't fully master.

Grant's jaw hung open with shock. Slowly, he raised

his wine glass to Brea and said, "To your first day back home, Brea."

Brea raised her glass and clinked it against his and Oriana's. "It's been an emotional day."

"I have so many questions," Grant said, palming the back of his neck. "You left when you were a very young woman. But why? Did you hate the United States? Did you just want to go on an adventure?"

Brea's eyes flickered toward Oriana's. Something strange and cold dropped into the base of her gut.

"My husband died," Brea explained. "And my career had fallen off the rails. I didn't know where to go or what to do, so I left."

"That must have been very hard," Grant said.

Suddenly, Oriana was struck with the realization that although they were still relative strangers, Grant was her older brother, a man who would want to protect her in any other reality. The fact that he wasn't Reese was a blessing, in a way. Oriana had technically lied to Reese all these years about her past, but Grant hadn't known anything about it. Which meant Grant wouldn't judge her as harshly. She hoped.

So, Oriana heard herself say, "We've gotten ourselves involved in a terrible situation, Grant." Her tone was very stern and dark.

Brea gave her a look of shock.

"We need advice," Oriana breathed. "I don't know who else to talk to. And the end of September is right around the corner."

Brea shrugged and dropped her chin, clearly at a loss.

Grant studied Oriana curiously. "I have a hunch this has nothing to do with art dealing."

"It's art dealing adjacent," Oriana said, her shoulders

sagging forward. "And I don't want to be too explicit. But Brea and I are responsible for something that happened back in 1998. We didn't think anyone else knew about it but us. That is until the beginning of September, when I began receiving messages from a stranger. They've threatened that they know what we've done and are demanding an obscene amount of money to keep quiet."

Grant crossed his arms over his chest. His face was stoic yet not judgmental. Oriana had a strange hunch he'd been blackmailed before in his own business dealings, but she wasn't sure why.

"I imagine that whatever this person knows wouldn't be good for either of your careers." Grant arched his eyebrows, catching on quickly.

"Not in the slightest," Oriana answered.

Grant sighed deeply. "I suppose this is the reason for your reunion?"

Oriana and Brea nodded.

"Right. Well. I'm sure this is a particularly anxious time for you both."

Oriana felt as though she hung onto his every word. Relief flooded through her chest, and she breathed easier, her lungs filling.

"Let me put you in contact with a private investigator," Grant began. "Roland and I have used him extensively over the years, and he always comes back with answers. Always. I mean, he will do anything."

Oriana stuttered. "I already have a great private investigator. She found Brea for me."

Grant tilted his head. "I see. Well. Just in case your investigator is no longer available, or you'd like to try our guy out, I'll leave his name and number here for you. It's up to you."

Grant reached for a clean napkin and wrote out the private investigator's name and number, which he'd apparently memorized long ago.

"He must have been important to you over the years," Oriana said.

"He really was," Grant said. "Back before the internet was up and running, it was much more difficult to know if anyone was telling the truth about who they were or what they were up to. Carl got us through the dark ages, if you will."

Oriana laughed glumly at his joke and took the napkin from Grant. "I can't thank you enough."

"Don't mention it. I hope this clears up soon."

Oriana's chin wiggled. "What would you suggest we do if we do track him down?"

"You're going to need to know his secrets," Grant explained with a sparkle in his eyes. "That's the only way he'll keep yours to himself."

Brea and Oriana made heavy eye contact, both stirring with the same questions: what "secrets" could this blackmailer possibly have? They didn't even know who he was. They couldn't dive through the events of the past and pinpoint his face.

That night, Oriana made a bed for Grant in the guest bedroom and said goodnight. Just before he shut the door, he nodded and said, "You're going to get through this, little sis. I know we don't know each other well, but you have that Coleman strength. Roland and I both see it." He paused, his eyes roaming along the carpet. "I'm sorry it took us so long to come together. But maybe the timing was just right so that we can help you with this terrible predicament."

Oriana's heart felt bludgeoned. "Thank you, Grant. Maybe you're right. I hope you are."

Downstairs, Oriana and Brea sat on the back porch, swaddled in blankets, staring out into the black night and listening to the ocean lap onto the sands. They were thousands of miles from where they'd done this in Thailand.

"It's selfish to think of my career, isn't it?" Oriana heard herself say, allowing herself the freedom of truth with her best friend. "I mean, I've had so much success. Much more than I probably deserved.

"I just can't help but think of Bernard Copperfield out in Nantucket. How beloved he was until, out of nowhere, he was accused of stealing all that money and sent to prison for twenty-five years. One minute, he was on top of the world, and the next, his family and all of his friends hated him. The difference is, of course, that I'm responsible," Oriana went on. "Bernard always knew he was innocent, but I've always known I was guilty."

Brea furrowed her brow. "You're not guilty. I'm the one who traded out the painting. I'm the one who took the money."

"But when you told me the truth, I didn't try to fix it," Oriana said.

"You wanted to protect me," Brea breathed, reaching over to take Oriana's hand. After a long pause, she added, "I don't think you should be worried about what your friends and family think, if and when this comes out. They adore you. More than that, I think they'll agree with me when they say that a few random blotches of green and blue paint on a canvas shouldn't amount to such drama."

Oriana's jaw dropped with surprise, and suddenly, she cackled, her body shaking. Ultimately, she knew Brea was right. Her family and friends knew very little about art. They wouldn't turn their backs on her because of a mistake early in her career.

But she wasn't willing to give up on her career just yet. They had to track down this blackmailer. They had to stop this in its tracks.

Chapter Twenty One

The living room where Brea had found Kenny after he'd collapsed was now filled with people eating potato salad, pasta salad, and scones. Everyone was dressed in black suits and dresses. Everyone looked forlorn, with their skin very pale due to the winter months and their cheeks slightly more plump than normal. It was the week between Christmas and New Year's, and everyone was just eating a little too much.

Brea felt disconnected from her body. As she made the rounds, adjusting the barrette in her hair, she heard herself thank people for coming, explaining she was doing all right but that it would be a hard road ahead.

Oriana was in the kitchen, spooning more salad into a large bowl, her face blotchy from crying. To her credit, Oriana had hardly left Brea's side since Kenny's death and had even spent the night at Brea's house on Christmas Eve, forcing her to watch old films and eat

Christmas cookies. It had been a brief light in the darkness for Brea.

"Hi, honey." Oriana washed and dried her hands and hugged Brea, her shoulders shaking. "I would ask you how you're doing again, but I'm even annoying myself at this point."

Reese appeared in the doorway, Alexa in his arms. Alexa rubbed her eye sleepily, and her hair was tousled, a big Christmas bow in the center. She hadn't been able to part with it since she'd removed it from one of her Christmas presents.

"Are you going to take her home?" Oriana asked.

"I think I'd better," Reese said. "Her stomach's still acting up."

"Poor baby." Oriana walked over to them and kissed Alexa on the forehead as Brea stirred with rage and jealousy. She and Kenny should have been allowed that dynamic. They should have had a baby; they should have supported one another in sickness and in health. They should have been something more.

After Reese took Alexa and Joel back home, Oriana poured Brea and herself a glass of wine and insisted Brea sit for a while. "You want something to eat? A cookie? A brownie? Something?" Oriana was well aware that Brea hadn't touched anything that morning, before or after the funeral.

"I'm not hungry," Brea said.

In the sitting room, which was a smaller enclave of the larger living room, Brea and Oriana sat side-by-side, sipping their wine and watching a soft snow fall out the front window. Brea felt as though she viewed her entire life through Saran Wrap, like everything was at a distance, foggy. When Oriana asked her questions, she usually had to ask her to repeat herself.

This was perhaps why when the man approached them and said her name, Brea didn't register it. Not at first.

Oriana leaped up to hug him, crying his name. Brea blinked at him, at the handsome Manhattan face, the sleek hair, and the sharp suit. It was Nick, Oriana's dear friend from the city. *Why was he here?*

"Brea," Nick began, his hand over his chest. "I am so sorry for your loss."

Brea stood on shaky legs and hugged him, remembering all the nights Nick had managed to "nix" Brea from club guest lists so that he could have Oriana all to himself. He'd seen Oriana as the heavier hitter in the art world, the one to know, while Brea had been just an intern. Why was he rubbing shoulders with Brea now? *Was it because of her recent high-figure art deals? Probably.*

"Thank you for coming," Oriana said, patting Nick's shoulder. "Can I get you something to eat? A drink?"

The sight of Nick shot adrenaline through Brea's system. Quietly, she followed behind them to the kitchen, where Oriana ordered Nick to update them on his life as she poured him a glass of scotch and prepared him a plate of food. Nick spoke of the city with tremendous love yet insisted that it wasn't half as good now that "his girls" were gone.

"Brea, you should come back to the city," Nick suggested. "Change things up for yourself and for your career."

Brea raised her shoulders. It wasn't the worst idea in the world, starting over. Then again, going back to the city meant reliving the trauma of Kenny's original illness and her quest to make money in any way possible. *What if she ran into Neal again?* Oh gosh. She just couldn't take it.

As Oriana finished Nick's plate, Brea was suddenly overcome with just how kind Oriana was, how giving. For more than two years, Brea had lied to her, manipulated her, and used her credentials to make herself a fat wad of cash. Oh gosh. She couldn't get over how wrong that was now.

And, perhaps because of her grief, insanity, or fear, Brea said, "Oriana? Can I talk to you? Maybe in the study?"

Oriana tilted her head but smiled a split-second later, eager to do whatever she could to make Brea's life easier. "Nick? Your plate's ready for you. Brea and I will be right back."

Brea led Oriana into the study and closed the door behind them. Sweat sprung up in her armpits, along her neck, and she paced nervously, willing herself to say the thing she'd come to say.

"Brea? What's going on?" Oriana was worried. Probably, she thought this was her friend's psychotic break at her husband's wake. She'd probably been expecting it.

Finally, Brea turned around, looked Oriana in the eye, and blurted, "I stole a painting from you to pay for Kenny's transplant."

Oriana's eye's widened in shock. Nobody spoke for a long, horrible moment, and Brea thought maybe she hadn't said anything, that she'd imagined it.

"What the hell are you talking about?" Oriana finally sputtered.

Brea raised her shoulders. "That first painting. The

four-million-dollar sale. The one you ultimately gave Walter was a forgery."

Oriana's face twisted with rage. "I don't understand. Brea? What are you saying?"

The self-hatred that Brea swirled in was no different than the self-hatred she'd felt since it had happened.

"For so long, I thought I'd done the right thing," Brea said. "Because Kenny got better, our careers took off, and then we moved here together. But now, Kenny is dead. And I don't imagine I'll ever want to sell a piece of art ever again. So." Brea clapped her thighs, realizing she'd just thrown their friendship off a cliff. There was no way it would survive this.

Oriana turned away from Brea, rasping into her hand. "I can't look at you right now." Her shoulders shook violently.

Brea's eyes were heavy with tears, so much so that she could hardly see through them. After she tried to sputter an apology, she fled the study, rushed through the kitchen, then went out the back door of her home, where she inhaled the ten-degree air and felt her tears against her cheeks. Oh, how she loved Oriana. Oh, how she loved this house and this island.

But at this moment, she knew she had to get as far away from Martha's Vineyard as she could. She would put the house on the market as soon as possible. It was the only way.

Chapter Twenty-Two

Present Day

The morning after Oriana and Brea returned from Thailand, a letter awaited on the front porch— this time addressed to both of them. Reese picked it up and put it on the breakfast table, smiling.

"Who's this from?"

Oriana grabbed it a little too quickly, searching for something to say. "It's probably from a friend of Brea's. We contacted a few people on our way back home."

"Everyone wants to welcome Brea back!" Reese said breezily as he opened up the newspaper. "I've missed her so much over the years. Doesn't having her around make you feel twenty-two again?"

Upstairs, Oriana and Brea locked Brea's guest room door and ripped open the envelope. The note said:

Not long now. Wait for instructions for the transfer on the first day of October. If the

money is not transferred, your secret will be revealed to everyone.

Brea's hand shook as she held the note. "This is so much creepier than I thought it would be."

Oriana understood what she meant. Blackmailers seemed theoretical, taken from crime thrillers or fantasy sagas.

"I'm going to contact Rita, my private investigator," Oriana said. "Now that Grant knows about the black-mailer, I feel safe telling one more person."

But Rita didn't pick up her phone this time. It rang multiple times and then went to voicemail. After Oriana tried a final time, she contacted Steve Montgomery about Rita, and he explained she'd gone to South America to work on a case and wouldn't be back for another couple of weeks at the earliest. Oriana's heart sank.

"Why don't we try Grant's guy?" Brea suggested.

"I guess it's our only option," Oriana agreed, leafing through her pocket to find the napkin upon which Grant had written the telephone number for Carl. It was only eight in the morning, but they were running short on time. The call had to happen now.

The phone rang three times before a man answered it. Immediately, a shiver of recognition went down Oriana's spine.

"Good morning. How may I help you?"

Oriana frowned. "Um. Carl?" But after a brief sputter, she added, "I'm sorry. You just sound so much like my friend Nick."

The open-hearted laughter on the other line confirmed that this was, in fact, Nick. "Oriana? Is that you?"

Brea's face echoed her panic and surprise, and Oriana's stomach twisted with a mix of confusion and joy. After all, she'd had marvelous times with Nick over the years. She'd even run into him recently at that party in Manhattan and felt she'd seen, within his eyes, so many long-lost nights with him, dancing in clubs, eating take-out, laughing.

"How did you get this number?" Nick asked.

"My uncle gave it to me," Oriana explained with the wave of her hand. "He said you sometimes work for him. As a private detective?"

Nick laughed again. "Yeah. You know me, Oriana. I always get carried away with my odd jobs. Private detective work has been my bread and butter for quite a while now. I love getting involved in other people's business."

"That does sound like you. You were always the biggest gossip in Manhattan."

"Unfortunately, I had to learn to keep people's secrets to myself unless someone shells out enough cash to hear them," Nick explained.

"Oh gosh. Wonderful." Oriana shook her head, still at a loss.

"So. I take it you wanted to hire a private detective?"

"Right. Yes." Oriana's thoughts spun. "Maybe we could talk about it in person? I don't love talking about it over the phone."

"Are you in the city?"

"I could be," Oriana said. "Time is of the essence. I could be there by tomorrow?"

"Sounds wonderful," Nick said. "Shall I text you an address and time?"

"That sounds great. And Nick?"

"What is it?"

"My uncle called you Carl. Isn't that strange?"

"It's better to be undercover," Nick explained. "My friends know me as Nick, but sometimes I have to investigate my friends. It's a tricky business. But somebody has to do it."

Oriana laughed again, and Nick joined in, and for a moment, Oriana could pretend that they were twenty-five again, up against the world in a pitch-black club as techno beats pumped through their bodies and they raised their arms to the sky.

After Oriana got off the phone, she had to face Brea, who looked as though she'd just seen a terrible accident.

"That was Nick?" she asked. "How is that possible?"

Oriana raised her shoulders. "Manhattan has gotten crazy expensive over the years. I guess he just picked up odd work for rich people."

Brea continued to frown at her, clearly uninterested in that explanation. "But isn't it a little too much of a coincidence?"

Oriana wasn't sure what Brea meant. But before she could answer, the doorbell rang downstairs, and Reese hollered up, "Meghan is here!"

A cold, hard stone fell into Oriana's gut. She realized she hadn't been in contact with her sister over the past few days— a result of her selfishness and fears. Brea's smile opened her face, and she scampered through the door and down the staircase with Oriana hot on her heels.

"Brea? Oh my gosh!" Meghan's jaw dropped.

As Brea swallowed Meghan in a hug, Oriana's knees wavered beneath her, threatening to give out. These were two of her favorite people in the world, genuinely overcome with joy at seeing one another again.

"What are you doing here?" Meghan asked, breathless. The door remained open behind her, and a cold autumn breeze wafted through.

Brea glanced back at Oriana, who remained on the staircase. "Oriana came and dragged me out of Thailand."

Meghan laughed gently. Her eyes were filled with forgiveness as she recognized Oriana had had quite a bit on her plate. She didn't even know the half of it.

"Do you want a cup of coffee?" Oriana asked with her hand around her throat. "Brea and I have something to tell you."

Meghan's shoulders dropped forward. All she'd wanted all these years was Oriana's honesty and her friendship. All she'd wanted was to support her.

Oriana should have told her everything about the blackmailer from the start.

* * *

Over the next hour, locked away in the guest bedroom, Oriana and Brea explained everything about the years between 1998 and 2000 to Meghan, along with the updated information from the previous few weeks. Meghan sat wide-eyed, not touching her coffee, her arms crossed over her chest.

"And then, Oriana just called Grant's private detective, and it was a guy we knew back in Manhattan," Brea finished. "I mean, that's weird, right?"

"It's really weird." Meghan's eyes glinted with intrigue. "Have you told Grant about that?"

"It just happened before you got here," Oriana explained. "But I don't think it's anything to worry about. Nick is just that kind of guy, you know? I used to run into him all over the city. I just did, in fact, at that party earlier this month. He knows everyone, makes money however he can, that kind of thing."

Meghan and Brea gave one another doubtful glances.

"I have a suggestion," Meghan said. "Why don't we go to Nantucket and explain what you just learned about Nick to Grant? Maybe he'll have more information about him."

"Information that either clears his name or..." Brea began as Oriana waved her hands.

"I don't think Nick did anything wrong. He's just a money guy," Oriana said. "But okay. Let's go to Nantucket. Why not?" She eyed Brea. "If anything, it's just part of the grand, 'Welcome back to the United States, Brea!' Tour."

"Glad to join up," Meghan quipped.

After a series of text messages with Grant, it was decided that they would meet at Roland's home early evening for dinner with the two brothers. Oriana and Brea decided to pack for the trip to New York and leave from Nantucket the following day; Meghan insisted on going with them and immediately went home to pack her own bag.

"We've carried this secret for decades," Oriana said. "And now, it seems like everyone and their mother knows about it."

"Not Reese," Brea reminded her.

Oriana's heart dropped into her gut. "I can't tell him now. I don't know what he'll say. If he reacts negatively, I don't want to have to think about it throughout the trip to Nantucket and the city." After another pause, she added, "But you're right. I should tell him."

"He would want to know," Brea told her.

"Did you ever tell Kenny?"

Brea shook her head. "But I was living in a fantasy world. I thought everything had turned out all right."

Oriana drove Meghan and Brea toward the Edgartown docks, where a ferry picked them up and sailed them over to Nantucket. By five-thirty, the three of them were at the front door of the massive Coleman Family House— an estate, more like.

"We didn't bring anything!" Meghan hissed. "Not even a bottle of wine!"

Oriana and Brea glanced at one another and burst into nervous giggles. Bringing something for dinner had been the very last thing on their minds. Before they finished laughing, Estelle opened the door and smiled at them confusedly.

"Well, hello! To what do we owe this spontaneous dinner?" Estelle beamed.

"It's just about the silliest thing," Oriana explained, dropping down to hug her half-sister-in-law. "I would tell you if it weren't so embarrassing."

Estelle set the table for Roland, Grant, his wife, Katrina, Meghan, Brea, Oriana, and herself. Dinner was an Indian lamb curry, and the spices of ginger and turmeric were warm and inviting.

"Did you ever go to India while you lived in Asia?" Estelle asked Brea as she poured them each a glass of red wine.

"I never did," Brea said. "I was on a small island and hardly left it."

"It sounds like paradise," Roland boomed as he entered the dining room, extending a hand for Brea to shake. "Grant told me all about you." His eyes flickered in a way that proved Grant had told him even more— all about the blackmailing.

But Oriana didn't see it as a betrayal. Rather, it was good that Roland already knew so that they could get the conversation going.

First, however, they ate. They piled their plates high with spicy meat, rice, and naan bread, swapped stories from their travels, and built a rapport that Oriana felt drew them closer together as a family. She knew it would take time to feel close to Roland and Grant, but now her heart opened wider to the idea of loving them completely.

When Estelle and Katrina left to wash the dishes in the next room, Oriana knew it was time to act.

"So." Grant crossed his hands over the table. "You mentioned you had something to discuss with us. Is this about what we talked about yesterday?"

Oriana nodded. "I contacted your private investigator. Ours wasn't available. Thank you again for passing his name along."

"He's the best in the business," Grant assured her. "Roland and I have used him numerous times."

"See, that's the weird thing about it," Oriana went on. "Because the minute your private detective answered the phone, I realized I knew him. We were very good friends back in New York in the late nineties and early two-thousands."

Grant's eyes widened. "You're kidding."

"It can't be a coincidence," Brea interjected.

"How did you meet Carl?" Grant asked.

"He was never Carl to me," Oriana went on. "His name was always Nick. But now that I think about it, it's not like I ever looked at his birth certificate. Maybe Carl is his real name, and Nick is his public name. I don't know."

"Strange. I guess it's important to keep both personas separate," Grant said thoughtfully.

But suddenly, Brea raised her hand and glared at Roland. "What is going on?" she demanded, her tone icy.

Oriana followed Brea's gaze to Roland, whose face had turned beet red. His eyes were blotchy, and he looked on the edge of having a breakdown. Even Grant was surprised at his brother's transformation.

"Roland? Are you all right?" Grant asked.

Roland grabbed a clean napkin and placed it over his mouth. His shoulders quaked violently. Something was very wrong.

Nobody spoke for a long time until Roland removed his napkin, looked Oriana dead in the eye, and said something that nearly crushed her.

"I hired Carl to tail you back in the late nineties."

Oriana, Brea, and Meghan were speechless. Oriana pressed her hand against her chest, struggling to breathe. All those years, Roland had pretended not to want anything to do with his sisters— yet he'd gone behind their backs, spying on them, to learn more.

All Oriana could think to ask was, "Why? Why would you do something like that?"

Roland sputtered. "I was curious, I guess. Interested in what you were up to in the city. I was too scared to reach out to you, but I wanted to know what you were like, how your career was going. The internet didn't exist back then, not in the same way. And you just couldn't learn about people unless..." He trailed off. "You said he befriended you?"

"We went everywhere together," Oriana rasped, feeling the worst sense of betrayal. "Nick, Carl, or whoever he was, went out with me all the time. We met important people and networked."

Oriana's head spun with images of Nick all those years ago: her handsome, wonderful, vivacious friend. He'd had dreams and visions for his life, and they'd spoken of them endlessly, with Oriana frequently giving him advice and ideas on how to proceed.

All that time, he'd been watching her.

"I never told him to do that," Roland said, his cheeks blotchy with rage. "That is completely unprofessional."

"They went everywhere together," Brea added, furrowing her brow. Suddenly, stricken, she gripped Oriana's wrist on the tabletop and cried out, "He was at Kenny's funeral!"

Oriana stuttered, staring into Brea's eyes. Immediately, she was taken back to that horrific day, the very last she'd seen her best friend before Brea had taken off. It had been the day Brea had told her about the forgery.

"He must have heard us talking," Brea whispered. "He knows."

Oriana and Brea turned back to stare at Roland, who still looked shell-shocked, heavy with shame.

"When was that funeral?" Roland asked.

"December 28, 2000," Brea answered.

Oriana's brain throbbed with this influx of information. *How could she put all the pieces together? How could they possibly make sense?*

But a moment later, she realized something.

"I didn't see Nick at all after that," she breathed. "Not till earlier this month— the day I started receiving the notes from the blackmailer."

"Oh my gosh." Meghan closed her eyes.

"I'm going to New York City to see him tomorrow,"

Oriana said. "But I don't know how to beat him at his own game. The end of the month is just a few days away."

Roland and Grant looked at one another gravely.

"Let us handle that part," Roland said. "I got you into this mess. Let us get you out of it."

Chapter Twenty-Three

As it turned out, Roland and Grant had another very good private detective connection— Rita, who was in South America but could pause for the night to do a few well-paid, hard-hitting hours studying Nick/Carl, or whatever his real name was. When Oriana learned they'd contacted Rita, she laughed and said, "She's my private detective!" To this, Roland and Grant sighed, with Grant saying, "Maybe you didn't need our help after all."

By the time everyone woke up at the Coleman family house the following morning, Rita had written back with an exposé of Nick/Carl's dealings over the years— and information about his real name.

Dear Roland, Grant, and Oriana,

It is much easier to research a man with arrogance, as he leaves clues about himself and his "true intentions" across the internet as a way to brag about how gifted and intelligent he is. I see it all over the world, in almost every case.

With that, I present to you the following:

Valentino Reggio. Originally born in Milan, Reggio came to New York as a teenager. He was penniless and worked as a pickpocket for a number of years until he met a young woman from a very wealthy family who fell in love with him. Naturally, he was charming, and he was able to rise in the ranks of her family until her father discovered he was stealing from him and kicked him out.

Around this time, he changed his name to Carl and began working as a private detective. Many people in New York City and surrounding areas used him, as he had a marvelous way of getting into other people's business. He was paid handsomely for his efforts, which led to suits, shoes, beautiful apartments, and vacations to Europe, all that jazz.

It seems that around 1999 or so, he started going by the name of Nick and hanging out with the artistic elite. In 2001, he began buying and dealing art— which, it seems, brought him great success for a period of time, that is, until recently.

According to several sources, most of the art Nick was dealing with were forgeries. Nick's career is on the brink of ruin, and he's had to pay millions of dollars to previous clients to shut them up and avoid going to prison.

Another source close to me, one I cannot reveal, tells a horrible story of Nick attempting to kidnap the son of a previous client and then returning him, pretending to have been the one who'd found him. This ultimately backfired. However, Nick knew enough about the client's backstory and illegal dealings that the client chose not to bring the story to the public eye.

In any case, this Nick/Carl/Valentino character seems terrible and potentially dangerous. Please, be careful in dealing with him.

Best,

Rita

Oriana read the email twice, trying to align this new version of reality with her old version. Roland and Grant were up in arms, with Grant calling Katrina at home and asking her to pack a bag for him. "I don't care what's in there. I'll be gone two days, maybe three."

"You're not going to New York on your own," Roland insisted as Grant blathered on. "We're all going with you."

"It's so bizarre, isn't it?" Brea said, crossing her arms over her chest. "He had this information in his back pocket for the past twenty-three years. Now that he's broke and in trouble, he decided it's time to use it."

"We won't let him," Meghan assured her.

Oriana eyed Roland and Grant nervously. After Grant got off the phone, she said, "Nick's been watching me the entire time. I mean, he knew where I was so often. Who's to say he doesn't know you're all in on it, now?"

"You're meeting him in the city today," Brea said. "He thinks you're coming to him for solace and help."

"That's right. My guess is he planned to charge you to 'hunt down' your blackmailer— and then double down on the blackmailing efforts later on," Roland said. "He had you cornered. Until now."

Oriana, Meghan, and Brea drove to the city in Oriana's car, while Roland and Grant took Roland's BMW. Throughout the drive, Brea flicked through radio stations nervously, and Meghan sighed occasionally, in a way that translated her fears and regrets and the horror of the entire operation. Oriana was speechless.

"I remember how you never liked Nick," Oriana said suddenly, her eyes flashing toward Brea in the front seat.

"I remember you asked me why Nick always had to come out with us."

Brea grimaced.

"You just didn't trust him?" Oriana asked.

"He wasn't like us," Brea said. "I mean, he just always seemed up to something. Besides, he never wanted me around. He wanted you to himself."

Oriana groaned and bounced her head on the seat rest. With all her strength, she wished she could go back in time and shake herself, to tell herself to be more aware of what was going on around her. More than anything, she wished she could scream at herself for her inability to see how much pain Brea had been in during the months Kenny had been so sick. Oriana had had her head in the clouds. She'd been a bad friend.

Nick had texted her an address and a time: his apartment at eight in the evening. Oriana and Roland valeted their vehicles at a garage down the road from the apartment building, then struck out— Oriana, Meghan, and Brea in front, and Roland and Grant staggered a bit behind.

The doorman of Nick's apartment building was expecting Oriana and even Brea, but he wasn't expecting anyone else. He insisted that only the two women could go up. Everyone else had to remain outside.

Oriana should have anticipated this. It was the way of these swanky apartment buildings in Manhattan.

"I'll come up with something," she muttered to Roland and Grant.

"Have us on speed dial," Grant urged her, then pointed to the Irish Pub across the street. "We'll be there, waiting."

"And we can call the police at any time," Roland assured her.

Oriana and Brea laced their fingers together and entered the lobby. Oriana could feel Brea's pulse fluttering in her wrist. As they rose through the heart of the building on the elevator, Oriana struggled to breathe. However, Brea locked eyes with her right before the doors opened into his penthouse suite and said, "We can do this. We're together again. And we know things that would destroy him."

Oriana knew she was right. But she couldn't trust Nick and had a hunch his slippery nature would help him evade them.

When the doors opened, Nick stood directly in the center of the foyer, his Italian suede shoes shining from the light of the chandelier and his smile sinfully handsome, fit for the cover of *GQ*. Oriana's heart flipped over with recognition. Her first instinct was to think: my friend!

"Oriana! Brea. So happy you could make it to the city today."

Oriana thought it was funny. She hadn't mentioned Brea at all on the phone with Nick yesterday. This was either a slip-up on his part or an acknowledgment that he knew she knew about his blackmail scheme. Oriana decided to tread lightly.

"Nicolas," Oriana said, rushing forward to hug him.

Brea walked up behind her, her smile wavering just slightly.

"Come on, Brea. Give us a hug." Nick waved his hand, and Brea sidled beside him, swatted his back, then stepped away.

"You were never particularly warm," Nick said with a laugh. "But I suppose we never really change, do we?"

Nick led Oriana and Brea to his state-of-the-art kitchen, where he poured them helpings of very expensive red wine and raised his glass. "To new beginnings," he said.

Oriana felt out of breath, on the verge of collapse. She heard herself echoing what he said, laughing at his jokes. But in reality, she felt as though she watched the entire exchange from above, as though it happened to someone else.

"So. Tell me." Nick leaned on the counter. "Why did you reach out to my private investigator persona? Who are you looking for?"

Oriana slid her tongue across her teeth. Around the kitchen were several expensive knives glinting ominously. Why wouldn't Nick murder them as a way to avoid having his secrets come to the surface? He had gone undercover before and changed his name. Surely, he could do it again. They had to find a way to get out of there.

"Let's not get into that just yet," Oriana said easily. "Do you have any idea how long it's been since I went out dancing?"

Nick's eyes widened, and he dropped his head back, laughing. "So, I take it your little problem doesn't have a time limit of some kind?"

"I'll tell you after we dance," Oriana said, trying to ensure her voice didn't waver. She guzzled half her glass of wine, thinking that the bottle had cost upwards of three hundred dollars. "Let's go, Nick! Don't tell me you can't get on those guest lists as easily as you used to."

It didn't take much more prodding to get Nick out of

the house. He was effervescent, excitable, like a golden retriever. As he changed clothes, Oriana sent Roland a text to pull the BMW around to the front of the building. She also said to leave Meghan at the Irish Pub because she didn't want her to be involved if she didn't have to be. This was Oriana's mess.

When they got into the elevator, Brea shot Oriana a confused look, but Oriana tried to flash her a smile of confidence. In reality, she wasn't sure if her plan would work. But gosh, it had to. It was a risk— and maybe their only shot.

As they stepped outside, the doorman said goodnight to Nick with a firm nod, and Oriana gestured toward the BMW on the curb.

"I called us an Uber already," she explained easily.

"Wow. A nice one!" Nick said, whipping toward it to open the back door for Brea, then Oriana to get in. As she did, she made eye contact with Roland in the rearview mirror as Nick leaped in happily, closed the door, and buckled his seatbelt. Apparently, Grant had also stayed at the Irish Pub— a good thing, too, as normally, Uber drivers didn't bring passengers. It could have been an indication something was off.

Immediately, Roland locked the doors. Oriana guessed he'd put the child security locks on the back door to ensure Nick couldn't leap out.

"All right! Let's get this show on the road," Nick said, clearly impatient.

But suddenly, Roland turned around and glared at Nick. All the color drained from Nick's face. At the door of his building, the doorman gaped at them, sensing something was wrong, and Oriana said, "You need to drive away, Roland. Drive!" So, Roland turned, started the engine, and drove away from the curb quietly until they reached the next road, where he turned and parked on the curb again.

By this time, Nick was pale and shaking.

"How are you doing, Carl?" Roland asked.

Nick flared his nostrils and tugged at the door latch, which didn't budge. "Let me out," he barked. "Immediately. Or I'll call—"

"The authorities? What are you going to tell them?" Roland demanded. "Are you going to explain how you've been blackmailing my sister the past month? Or are you going to tell them that you kidnapped someone's child, sold multiple forged paintings and sculptures, and switched identities at least two times? I imagine there are a number of tax evasions along with that list, but I digress."

Nick looked like he might throw up.

"None of this has to come to light, Valentino," Roland went on. "All you have to do is back off my sister, stop sending her terrifying messages, and stop demanding she pay you cash. And if I catch wind of you being so heinous to anyone else, I will not hesitate to send your name to the authorities."

"I'll take her down with me!" Nick barked.

"Right. Well, I think you kidnapping is much worse than her issue," Roland said, rolling his eyes. "You'll spend years in prison. Do you really want that?"

Nick very clearly did not want that. After a shuddering sigh, he stared at his shoes and said, "You have my word. I'll back off."

Oriana was heavy with disbelief.

"Do you believe him, Oriana?" Roland asked.

Oriana turned to gape at Brea, who was similarly

pale. This had been their trial for twenty-five years at this point, the horrific thing that had divided them and taken Brea across the world. *Would it all really end here, in the back of Roland's BMW? Was life really so strange?*

"Just get out of my life," Oriana finally muttered to Nick, disgusted with him. She didn't want to see him again.

Due to the child locks, Roland had to get out of the car, walk around, and let Nick out. When Nick scampered out, he stumbled on the curb and nearly fell on his face, which would have been the cherry on top.

"I cannot believe that worked," Brea whispered, dropping her head on Oriana's shoulder as Roland returned to the driver's side.

"He's a rat," Roland said. "And we just happened to have a rat trap all set up for him. Easy."

When they got back to the Irish Pub, Grant and Meghan leaped in the BMW, and Roland drove them away from Nick's building toward the Upper West Side. After Oriana explained everything that had happened, the five of them fell into a stunned but comfortable silence, on the other side of an explosive incident that had probably changed them for good.

All they could do now, they supposed, was eat the most sinfully delicious thing in all of Manhattan—Chinese food, or French food, or very expensive Mexican with plenty of melted cheese, and sleep in a hotel bed, dreaming of brighter tomorrows.

Chapter Twenty-Four

J ust four days after Oriana returned to Martha's Vineyard from New York City, Oriana received a phone call from Walter Billington's wife, Priscilla. It was so out of the blue, yet also so in tune with everything else that had been happening, that Oriana was immediately fearful that Walter had learned about the painting's forgery anyway and had decided to call to demand answers.

"Hi, Priscilla! How are you?" Oriana sat on the back porch of her home on a gorgeous early October day, watching as Brea and Benny played in the grass. Benny had really taken to her.

"Hello, Oriana. I'm so sorry to reach out like this. I wanted to let you know that Walter passed away in his sleep a few nights ago."

Oriana's heart dropped. "Oh no. Priscilla, I'm so sorry. Walter was a remarkable man."

Priscilla sounded resigned, her voice heavy with the tragedy of it all. "He always spoke of you so highly. Your friendship meant a lot to him."

Oriana pressed her hand on her forehead, unable to believe this. Walter had been a dashing man in his forties when she'd met him. How was it possible his life was already over?

"His friendship meant so much to me, too," Oriana stuttered. "Our conversations were some of the most important I ever had. He taught me so much about the world. About art and music."

"Yes. It's impossible to understand the fallout of his death right now." Priscilla sighed. "I never really understood that first painting you got him to buy. The one with the green and blue blotches?"

Oriana laughed gently. "I know the one."

"But he just adored it," Priscilla said. "He never let me move it anywhere else in the apartment. He said he saw something of himself in it. Something of a previous version, before time had its way with him. I suppose art does that to people. It creates a personal connection, even if others can't understand it."

Oriana blinked back tears, considering telling Priscilla the truth: that the painting had always been a forgery and that Walter had been wronged. That, worst of all, Oriana had known about it for twenty-three years.

But what good would that do? It would only irritate Priscilla. It would only make Walter out to be a fool.

And, beyond anything, hadn't that painting done its job? It had spoken to Walter for all these years. It had been a comfort as he'd aged. It had filled him with longing and love.

That meant it wasn't technically a forgery, not really. It was art in all the ways art was meant to be.

Oriana asked Priscilla to pass along details of the funeral. She wanted to come to pay her respects. After she got off the phone, she padded down the porch steps to find Brea and Benny on the grass, stretched out on the damp ground to stare at the cerulean blue. Oriana flounced down beside them and followed their gaze to watch a flock of birds in perfect V-formation headed south for the winter. It never ceased to amaze her.

"Walter Billington passed away," Oriana breathed to Brea, not quite loud enough for Benny to hear, as he was on the other side of Brea.

Brea frowned. "I'm so sorry to hear that."

"According to his wife, he loved that painting till the end."

Brea brushed a tear from her cheek and then propped herself up on her elbow, her face pained and serious. "I reached out to Rita the other day."

"What about?"

"I wanted to know what happened to the original painting," Brea said. "The one I swapped out. Poor Rita, we've used her so often the past few weeks. But it sounds like she's at a standstill on the situation in South America and was grateful to sink her teeth into something easier to track down.

"According to Rita, Neal sold the painting to a dealer in the Netherlands for five million dollars back in 1998. After that, it went off the grid for a while, then was sold in an auction for eight million in Tokyo in 2008."

"Wow," Oriana whispered, shaking her head.

"But in 2011, it was burnt to a crisp in a house fire," Brea went on. "Nobody was hurt, and the damage to the rest of the house was negligible. But that painting was taken. There's a rumor that the wife of the guy who purchased the painting had always hated it and set it on fire on purpose when she'd learned he was having an affair."

Oriana's lips formed an O. "What a story."

"That painting had serious power," Brea finished. "But now, that power is dead."

"It lives on in the forgery," Oriana said with a smile. "As long as Nick keeps the secret— and he will— the forgery will stake its claim as the world's only known painting of its kind."

Brea dropped back on the ground, so her salt and pepper hair wove through the grass. On the other side of her, Benny had dropped into sleep, and his eyes twitched behind the glow of his eyelids. Oriana felt a wave of impossible love for him.

"I'm going to start looking for a house here," Brea said. "I want to stay. If you think that's a good idea."

Oriana smiled and dropped her head on her best friend's shoulder. Another V-flock of ducks flew past, wings swaying through the breeze.

"I think it's a fantastic idea," Oriana whispered.

They'd already lost so much time. But, for reasons that now seemed mystical and outside of reason, Oriana and Brea had found a way back to one another again. It was up to them to electrify the rest of their days together on the island of Martha's Vineyard, even as the autumn sun died above them and cast them further toward the blissful and cozy months of frost.

Coming Next in the Coleman Series

Pre-Order Autumn Skies & Pumpkin Pies

Other Books by Katie Winters

The Vineyard Sunset Series

Secrets of Mackinac Island Series

Sisters of Edgartown Series

A Katama Bay Series

A Mount Desert Island Series

A Nantucket Sunset Series

Made in the USA
Monee, IL
15 November 2024

70226851R00118